D0707459

HOSPITAL HEARTBREAKER

After a happy start at Chad's, a big London hospital, things start to go wrong. Fleur meets surgeon Russell Delaney and unfounded rumours begin to sweep the wards. Fleur knows who is to blame. Yet, despite herself, she is irresistibly drawn towards the man who has broken so many fragile hearts amongst the hospital nursing staff and who, despite his preoccupation with the lovely Rowena Kingsley, seems determined to add hers to the list.

CALGARY PUBLIC LIBRARY

CALGARY PUBLIC LIBRARY

HOSPITAL HEARTBREAKER

Hospital Heartbreaker

by
Bridget Thorn

Dales Large Print Books
Long Preston, North Yorkshire,
England.

British Library Cataloguing in Publication Data.

Thorn, Bridget
 Hospital heartbreaker.

A catalogue record for this book is
available from the British Library

ISBN 1-85389-715-9 pbk

First published in Great Britain by Robert Hale, 1988

Copyright © 1988 by Bridget Thorn

Published in Large Print February, 1997 by arrangement
with Marina Oliver.

All rights reserved. No part of this publication may be
reproduced, stored in a retrieval system, or transmitted in any
form or by any means, electronic, mechanical, photocopying,
recording or otherwise, without the prior permission of the
Copyright owner.

Dales Large Print is an imprint of
Library Magna Books Ltd.
Printed and bound in Great Britain by
T.J. International Ltd., Cornwall, PL28 8RW.

ONE

Fleur paused in the doorway of the nurses' flats and groped in her bag for her umbrella. How different it was this morning, she thought with a sigh, pulling her cloak about her and setting off along the broad tree-lined path towards the hospital.

When she had last been on duty the autumn sun had been strong, a light breeze riffling the crisp brown leaves underfoot, and the faintest whiff of bonfires hanging in the air.

Now the raindrops dripped steadily from stark, menacing branches onto drifts of muddy, oozily glistening leaves, dank and ugly, dark clouds filled the sky, and the air was damp and cold instead of briskly invigorating.

Fleur sighed again. The weather mirrored her mood. In bright sun she would have been glad to leave St John's, the modern, busy midland hospital where she had trained and where, until recently, she had been so happy. Her sensible move to Chad's, a famous London hospital, good both for her career and her personal relationships, now seemed suspiciously like escape.

'Hi, Fleur, wait!' a voice called, and Fleur turned as she heard the light footsteps pounding along behind her.

'It's OK, Anne,' she said teasingly, 'you're not late.'

'Perhaps as well,' puffed the small dark girl. 'I don't want a reputation for unpunctuality to follow me. It's been an unfair handicap since my watch broke down on Prelim!'

Fleur laughed. 'And on first ward, and geriatrics, not to mention theatre,' she murmured provocatively. 'Nurse Fleet, I wish your actions were more in accord with your name!' she added, in imitation of the broad Scottish accent of the Senior Nursing Officer.

Anne Fleet groaned. 'That's been another handicap all my life. I came last even at playgroup, and have always been teased unmercifully about it. The sooner I change it the better. Let's hope there are eligible Registrars at Chad's.'

'I've had enough of men for a while,'

Fleur replied as lightly as she could and Anne, aware that her remarks had been slightly tactless, hastily changed the subject.

'I'm looking forward to our flat,' she said. 'I still think I'm dreaming, it's so close to the hospital, and convenient to tubes and everything. Only fifteen minutes to Oxford Street! Think of all those West End shops, and the clothes!'

'And the prices,' Fleur said dryly. 'We're paying more rent than we thought and won't have much to spare for clothes.'

She recalled how thankful she'd been when Anne had applied for a course at Chad's. It would make so much difference to be with an old friend, and she and Anne had been at school together before starting their training, so knew one another well.

'We can always find a third girl. I wouldn't mind that tiny boxroom, there's just room for a bed.'

'But not all your clothes.'

Anne giggled. She was notorious for snapping up bargains in all the sales, and even at jumble sales held by the League of Hospital Friends. Many she never wore, but was always happy to lend them to her friends when they were desperate for a new top or a different party dress.

'I'm having a throwing out session tonight,' she promised, and Fleur chuckled. The only clothes to be discarded would be too small, or so disreputable as to be beyond repair.

'See you at lunch if Sister will let me go at twelve,' she replied, and waved as she turned down a side path towards Men's Medical, set in one of the side wings of this sprawling building.

Chad's would be different, she mused. No edge of town green field site for the busy London hospital, crammed in between row after row of offices and houses. At least there was a large park nearby, she reminded herself, recalling her only previous visit. It would be something to remind her of the country.

A few minutes later she walked into the ward and smiled inwardly as Sister Beasley glanced at her watch. She took care never to give Sister cause for genuine complaint, and had only two more days to endure the hostility of the older girl.

'Staff Nurse Tremaine, there's a new patient in the side ward, suspected concussion. Make him comfortable first,' she said sharply, and turned to snap a reprimand at a student who was fiddling with her insecurely attached hat.

Fleur, reprehensibly, winked at the student who smothered a giggle, and went to the side wards, small rooms opening from a corridor beyond the main ward.

The first two contained old patients, Fleur saw, glancing through the observation windows in the doors. She had almost reached the second pair when she halted abruptly.

One of the doors had opened and a tall, thin-faced nurse emerged. She glanced smugly at Fleur and paused.

'I thought you'd moved to Casualty,' Fleur exclaimed.

'Only temporarily,' the other replied. 'I'm having your job, so they sent me back early. I wonder how you'll make out at Chad's? They have very high standards there.'

Fleur, with a great effort, remained silent. She suspected most of her problems arose from the envy and malice of Liza Price, but she could prove nothing. It would serve no purpose to quarrel. She turned away, but Liza came close beside her.

'Your new patient is in room four,' she

said loudly. 'Just the right type for you, Nurse Flirt!'

Clenching her hands and gritting her teeth, Fleur ignored this jibe. Pretty, lively, popular with patients and male staff, the pun on her name had at first seemed rather a joke. Now, though, after the unfair accusations that had poisoned the last few months, she found it hard to remain silent as her tormenter deliberately tried to provoke her.

She turned abruptly towards room four, where the door was slightly open. Without glancing through the observation she marched straight in. Liza behind her gave a low laugh, then Fleur's attention was fully taken up with the man on the bed.

'No, you mustn't,' she exclaimed, moving swiftly towards him and putting a hand on his shoulder.

He was sitting on the side of the bed, bending over the locker, obviously searching for something in it. The regulation hospital pyjamas had been tossed into the corner of the room and all Fleur could see of her new patient was a head of ruffled dark hair, crisp and wavy and slightly long, broad muscular shoulders, a long bronzed back and slim athletic hips.

A tremor, probably alarm, shook her as she touched him. She had an inexplicable urge to snatch her tingling fingers away from his smooth, firm flesh. No patient with suspected concussion should be moving about, she thought dazedly. He might be perfectly all right, but until the tests had been completed no chances should be taken.

'You must lie down,' she ordered firmly, and tried to push him down onto the pillows. He ignored her totally and her hands met only resistance. She might have been invisible and utterly helpless. She pushed more strongly, but achieved nothing apart from an irritable shrugging of his shoulders. At least he knew she was there, she thought ruefully, and then jumped as he spoke.

'Where the hell are my clothes?' a deep voice demanded, and Fleur found herself looking down into furious blue eyes that were deep set in a hard, strong, tanned face.

'You can't leave here yet,' Fleur said as soothingly as she could, trying to stop her voice from shaking. It was utterly ridiculous that she, a nurse two years qualified, should be made to feel like a trembling student just because an arrogant patient snapped her head off. 'There are tests to complete, and meanwhile you must stay in bed. I'll wash and shave you—'

'The devil you will!' the patient interrupted furiously, beginning to rise to his feet. Then, as he became aware of his state of nudity, he grinned disarmingly at her, his eyes changing from glittering, hard flints to twinkling sapphires. Decorously, but utterly without embarrassment, he draped the sheets about him as he subsided back onto the side of the bed.

'You may have concussion,' Fleur struggled to control her trembling voice. 'You must rest until we have all the results.'

'Crazy! I haven't got concussion. My brain is working perfectly adequately to confirm that without a scan and a battery of temperature charts,' he replied scathingly. 'But if you're going to be my nurse I'm willing to stay in bed, though I'm damned if you're going to shave me! Other attentions I might appreciate, if you live up to your name, Nurse Flirt,' he added outrageously, and Fleur's cheeks flamed.

'I'm Staff Nurse Tremaine,' she retorted angrily, turning to retrieve the pyjamas from the floor. 'Please put them back on,' she said in her frostiest and bossiest tone, but he made no move to take them from her outstretched hand.

'You look even prettier when you're angry, cheeks the colour of damask roses,' he remarked coolly. 'Honey blonde, big green eyes, eminently kissable lips, and,' he added musingly as he let his gaze wander lingeringly and appreciatively down towards her small and shapely but sensibly shod feet, 'the sort of long legs and delectably tempting figure to drive a man wild.'

'Your pyjamas!' Fleur said furiously, struggling to retain some composure under his insultingly candid regard.

He grinned and leaned back on one elbow.

'I'm feeling weak suddenly,' he remarked, with a gleam in his eyes, but his voice was as strong as ever. Fleur gritted her teeth. 'You'll have to help me.'

Fleur was about to refuse, then her professional training came to her rescue. Forcing herself to control the sudden trembling that gripped her limbs she stepped closer, and held the jacket open. Then, realising that he had no intention of helping her, she took the nearest arm and thrust it, much less gently than she would normally have done, through the sleeve.

He looked at her, his eyes narrowed into slits as she paused before reaching to take the arm he was propping himself upon. To grasp it she had to lean across him. Though he was leaning backwards she felt his muscles tense as she removed his prop, and he held himself rigid until she had struggled to pull on the other sleeve. Then, so suddenly that she could do nothing to prevent it, he flopped against the pillows and his arms, hard, strong and determined, had pulled her on top of him.

Fleur forgot everything as she struggled, panic-stricken, to release herself, but he had imprisoned her arms within his own, and however hard she twisted away from him she could do nothing to prevent his lips, hard and warm, claiming hers as he put one hand behind her head and forced her mouth down to his.

She felt giddy, her senses almost leaving her as she lay on top of his hard body, his lips teasing hers into submission and instinctive response. Her heart was pounding, her thoughts in complete con-fusion, Fleur was shamingly aware of the sudden almost overwhelming desire to submit to him which surged through her body, and she redoubled her efforts to free herself.

At last he paused for breath, and his eyes laughed up at her as he finally released her.

'Mm, delicious, like nectar,' he murmured, and remained smiling as Fleur, all her training and consideration for patients driven out of her thoughts, dealt him a stinging slap on the cheeks as she scrambled shakily from the bed.

'Staff Nurse Tremaine!'

Fleur turned, flushed, dishevelled, and furious, to see Sister Beasley standing in the doorway. Even though her eyes gleamed with satisfaction at having, this time, caught Fleur behaving badly, she looked genuinely shocked.

'This—fraud—is no more concussed than I am!' Fleur said furiously. 'I want to make a complaint! He assaulted me!'

'Wait in my office, Staff!' Sister cut in sharply. 'Your reputation won't be enhanced by this episode. Staff Nurse Price will take over your duties.'

Dismayed, Fleur noticed Liza Price behind Sister, openly gloating at her discomfiture. Now there would be no chance of forgetting. Before lunchtime the whole of the hospital would know, or at least would have heard the very biased version which Liza and Sister would spread.

She began to protest, then shrugged and brushed past Liza. Her eyes were misting and she did not see the curious glances of the nurses as she marched, stony faced, cap and hair awry, but with her head thrown high, to the office and waited for Sister Beasley.

While she waited she resolved not to plead with the woman who hated her. She was bound to be called to the Senior Nursing Officer for a reprimand, and she would explain to her.

Whether she would be believed was another matter, but despite vague accusations of undue friendliness and worse with male patients, Sister had never been able to substantiate her insinuations. Fleur's only previous interview with the Senior Nursing Officer had ended inconclusively, without a reprimand or warning to mar her record, but she had the distinct feeling that the elderly Miss Jackson considered that only definite proof of Sister's charges was lacking. This time, innocent as she was, circumstances would be against her.

'I don't want to hear your excuses,' Sister Beasley announced a few minutes later, after she had taken a seat behind her desk and looked at Fleur with ill-concealed triumph. 'I am sending you off duty in the ward, but you are to remain in your room and wait to be called to see Miss Jackson. It's a great pity that your time here should end so appallingly, but no more than I expected,' Sister added gloatingly, and Fleur had to make a great effort not to commit a genuine offence by telling the older girl exactly what she thought of her.

She left the office silently, and gained some slight satisfaction at Sister's frustrated look. Without speaking to any of the other nurses—they would soon know what had happened, though it would no doubt be a totally incorrect version—she walked out and went back to the small studio flat which had been her home since she had arrived at the hospital, fresh from school and eager to follow her chosen career.

She made coffee but could not drink it. She began to pack her cases, thankful to be leaving soon, but furiously angry that it should be in such a manner. She liked St John's, and got on well with most of the staff. There had been trouble only with Liza Price, resentful that so often Fleur had beaten her to the top place in examinations, and Sister Beasley, who had taken over Men's Medical a few months previously.

'They're jealous cats!' Anne declared when she rushed in, having sacrificed her lunch break to come and discover the truth of the rumours flying about the hospital. 'It's so unfair, that you should be punished for what that dreadful man did,' she went on as she made tea and tried to persuade Fleur to eat.

'At least they can't sack me,' Fleur attempted to joke.

'No, but gossip spreads, even to Chad's,' Anne said. 'If you won't eat I'll have some biscuits. Beastly Beasley says you're leaving to follow Steve Markham.'

'She's said that since I handed in my notice,' Fleur replied, 'and it's not true. I didn't know he'd gone to Chad's until after I got the job. We didn't keep in touch.'

'She won't believe that, she was so mad when he took you out. Before that she considered him her property.'

'If it would help, I wish I could give him to her! I don't know whether I dislike men or women most at this moment!'

'It's when they get together, or don't, that there's trouble. At least you'll be working on a women's ward at Chad's.'

'I should have applied to an all-women hospital, there'll still be too many men around for my liking,' was all Fleur would reply, and soon afterwards Anne had to leave to go back on duty.

'Please eat something,' she begged. 'I'll contradict Liza and La Beasley. When do you see the SNO?'

'I haven't been summoned. Thanks, Anne,' she added.

People would not believe Anne, Fleur thought gloomily, since her friend would be expected to support her. But she wished Miss Jackson would call her. This waiting, not knowing what was happening, was unbearable.

Some hours later she had still heard nothing. She was pacing up and down the small room, when she heard running feet in the corridor.

The door burst open and Anne almost fell into the room.

'Here, a note Beasley asked me to bring you,' she gasped, thrusting a sealed envelope at Fleur. 'Open it, quickly.'

Her hands shaking slightly, Fleur did so and read the brief missive inside. Then she looked up, her green eyes puzzled.

'I'm to report for duty in the morning as usual,' she said slowly. 'Anne, what does it mean?'

'She's decided to forget it?' Anne queried, astounded. 'La Beasley? When she had what she must have thought was a genuine complaint, even though we know the truth? I don't believe it!'

'What else does it mean? If she had reported me the SNO would have interviewed me before I was allowed back.'

'Perhaps your concussed admirer confessed?' Anne suggested.

'She wouldn't have believed him, even if he were the sort of man to admit a fault!' Fleur said sharply. 'I don't understand.'

'No need to. Come on, get changed, we'll go and have a huge meal at Giovanni's. I'm starving, and it will be the last time! There's the party tomorrow night.'

TWO

The female surgical ward at Chad's was a busy, friendly place. Fleur was welcomed eagerly, since they had been understaffed for months. The regular staff were a happy, efficient team, and within days she felt thoroughly at home.

'I'm so glad I chose theatre,' Anne said one morning, 'but I can't wait to meet the fabulous Russell Delaney. Have you seen him yet?'

'No. The professional hospital heart breaker, I heard.'

'He's been in Edinburgh, due back a couple of days ago. A brilliant surgeon though he's only in his early thirties. Tipped for a consultancy before he's forty.'

'He doesn't sound good husband material, with his reputation,' Fleur warned. Anne, though an excellent and dedicated nurse, longed to marry and have a family.

Now she gave a shamefaced laugh.

'Oh, no, I'm not stupid. Actually, one of the housemen, David Willis, is rather nice. We're going out tonight. I'm curious to see a man who sends all the nurses into flat spins.'

'I can do without, thanks,' Fleur said and changed the subject, suggesting they went shopping for curtain material.

'I won't put up with that awful dingy cream stuff a moment longer than I have to.'

Later, when Anne and David, a large, pleasant, cheerful young man who had trained at Chad's and was a star player in its Rugger team, had gone, Fleur admitted to herself that she was afraid of meeting the renowned Russell Delaney.

Since the episode with the good looking patient, and her own instinctive response, Fleur had been both puzzled and worried. Pretty and popular, she'd had many boyfriends and fancied herself in love. But no-one's kisses had sent such quivering waves of desire coursing through her body.

The circumstances had been unusual, she told herself, and also unexpected, so that her chemical reaction had been partly to blame for the nervous fears she had experienced. Yet the image of that handsome face with its deep set eyes persisted, as did that of his naked torso, and the recollected feel of his hard muscular body. He had undoubtedly been the most handsome man she had ever encountered, and she was secretly afraid that it had been the sheer good looks of the man which had stimulated her instinctive response.

Fleur had always been unusually responsive to beauty, in music or painting, the perfection of a flower or the charm of a young animal. Her mobile lips had always curved into a smile as she appreciated some delight of form or sound, and now she was beginning to fear that masculine beauty was having the same sort of effect on her. It could create enormous problems, and she had no wish to meet avowedly handsome men.

That was not a problem with Steve Markham, she conceded the following day, when she met him for the first time at Chad's.

He was large, with a square, pale face, prominent pale grey eyes and, though only in his late thirties, his fair hair was receding rapidly. He usually dressed in shabby old tweeds, good quality but poorly fitting, maintaining that physical comfort was of far greater importance than sartorial elegance.

Plain, comfortable and nice, was the usual verdict of nurses skilled in categorising the male staff, and Fleur agreed. Friendly and undemanding, he was a pleasant escort, but there had never been anything deeper between them than mutual liking.

Steve was now a Registrar at Chad's, on the firm of a consultant who specialised in abdominal surgery, and Fleur knew she would meet him on her new ward. However, it was in the canteen when she was taking a hasty lunch that she saw him.

He was sitting with a couple of older men at a table nearby, his back to her, wearing a familiar worn tweed jacket and drill trousers. She did not think he had seen her until the others got up to leave and he came across to sit opposite her.

'Welcome to Chad's. I heard you'd arrived. Glad to see you again, Fleur. What do you think of us?'

'I wonder why I didn't come here years ago,' Fleur replied. 'Everyone's so friendly. I suppose I was reluctant to leave St John's as I knew it, and had enjoyed my training so much.'

Steve nodded. 'I know what you mean. But you'll like Chad's even more. We have rarer cases, of course, being a London hospital, and that's a challenge, as I'm finding.'

They discussed one of the patients Steve was interested in, a woman with severe jaundice who had been admitted to Fleur's ward that morning, and as he rose to leave her he said that he would be popping up to see the woman later on.

'If you're not too busy settling in, perhaps you'll have a drink with me this evening?' he asked.

'Thanks, I'd like that.'

'The Crown is the favourite local.'

'I've seen,' Fleur replied. 'It even has a garden!'

'Not for this time of year,' Steve said, shivering. It had become really cold the last few days. 'In good weather you can't move outside for the crowd. When do you finish?'

'I'm off at five today.'

'Right, see you over there as soon as you can make it.'

The afternoon was uneventful, routine tasks, until Fleur was checking her patients before she went off duty. Then she noticed that one of the drips had been badly connected and there were small bubbles of air in the tube.

Swiftly she dealt with this, waited to ensure that no more bubbles had crept into the tube, and then, seeing that Sister was talking to one of the consultants in her office, went to find the student who had been responsible for changing the drip.

She found her in the ward kitchen, making coffee and setting out a tray with two cups and a plate of chocolate biscuits. Another cup, half full, was on the table, and as Fleur walked in she reached for it and took a swift mouthful.

'Nurse Massingham!' Fleur said sharply, and Gilly Massingham turned guiltily towards her. 'Did Sister tell you to have your coffee break here?' Fleur asked curtly.

'No, but it's two hours since I had a break,' the girl, a second year student, said sulkily. 'I didn't think there was any harm in it while I was making some for Sister and Mr Rogers.'

'It happens to be against the rules. But that wasn't what I wanted. Did you change Miss Porchester's drip?'

'Yes. Why?'

Frowning at the insolent tone she used Fleur spoke sharply.

'You ought to be capable by now of ensuring that no bubbles of air get into the drips. Don't you realise just 30 mls could be fatal? It's not a difficult job, just needs care and concentration. If you can't achieve these you won't make a very successful nurse.'

'There weren't any bubbles when I last looked!'

'Then how did they get there? You're responsible for that drip. I hope you're not being silly enough to accuse anyone else of interfering with it. Sister must be told. We can't allow nurses to be careless and pay so little attention to a patient's welfare. Now take in the tray and make sure you're more careful in future.'

With an angry glance from under her lashes, the girl turned away from Fleur, and in a defiant gesture suddenly picked up her cup and finished the coffee she had been drinking. Fleur gritted her teeth, but said no more, merely waiting until she had carried the tray into sister's office.

'She isn't the best of students,' Sister Reynolds said later when Fleur reported the incident. 'She came here thinking she knew everything, according to her tutor. On the basis, I think, of having read a simple textbook. We must keep an eye on her.'

When she came off duty Fleur changed rapidly into a warm skirt of a rich golden brown, and a thick, polo-necked, darker brown sweater. It promised to be a hard winter, she thought, and already she had begun to wear boots even on her short journeys between the flat and Chad's. She tugged on some elegant long suede ones, dark brown and high heeled, and clasped a matching belt about her slender waist.

As she brushed her dark blonde hair loose she surveyed her reflection critically in the locker room mirror and then nodded to herself. The sweater had been the right shade after all. When she had bought it she had been tempted by one of a lighter colour, but this enhanced the brightness of her shoulder-length hair, falling with a slight wave over the collar of the sweater.

She put on a discreet lip gloss, and then shrugged into a thick, warm sheepskin jacket. If the weather got colder still she would have to buy herself a warm coat for days when even this jacket was not enough.

The Crown was opposite the main entrance to the hospital, and there were only a few people there, none of whom Fleur recognised.

She sat where she could see the doors, and looked round her appreciatively at the opulence of the solid Victorian interior.

To one side were a series of booths, separated by high wooden partitions topped with panels of decorative multi coloured glass. The wood was real rich mahogany, lots of it and worn smooth and glossy with time, polish and loving care.

That, the heavy dark green and gold flocked wallpaper, and faded prints of various nineteenth century sporting events, were reflected in the yards of bright mirrors behind the bar, their coloured borders echoing the pattern in the glass partitions.

Several times the doors swung open to admit more customers. Four nurses Fleur knew came in with boy friends, and waved as they crowded into one of the booths. Then the doors swung open again and Fleur stiffened with shock as she saw a woman, tall and elegant, swathed in furs, and a man in evening dress.

As though hypnotised, Fleur watched him settle his companion at a small table

31

before going to the bar, then she turned to hide her face. What could he be doing here, of all places?

The memory of that disastrous episode swept over her again, as it did several times each day, but now the man involved was sitting a few feet away from her with one of the loveliest, sophisticated, and most expensively dressed women Fleur had ever seen. She knew she was blushing as she recalled the touch of his bare skin and muscular body, and the searing kiss he had forced upon her.

To her immense relief the couple had just the one drink and then, after glancing at their watches, left. She breathed deeply, trying to calm her tumultuous emotions, and did not see Steve until he dropped into a seat beside her.

'Sorry, I didn't mean to be so late, but there was an emergency peritonitis. Only just got away.'

Fleur replied disjointedly, and instead of the wine she would normally drink, surprised Steve by asking for a whisky.

'Not much soda, no ice,' she added, and he raised his eyebrows slightly.

'Had a hard day?' he asked sympathetically.

'What? Oh, middling,' she replied, and then forced herself to pay attention to him by asking questions about the hospital.

He replied patiently, but she had great difficulty in concentrating. What had that wretched man been doing here? Was it chance that he had come into this pub, or did he live or work nearby? Angrily she tried to dismiss the disturbing recollections his appearance had conjured up in her mind, but his face persisted in forcing itself onto her attention.

'I'm sorry, what was that?' she had to ask Steve.

'I was wondering if you'd like to have dinner with me. There's a very good Italian place a couple of blocks away.'

Fleur shook her head.

'Sorry, Steve, I'm too tired. I'm not very good company at the moment. I ought to have an early night.'

'You do look pale,' he commented, concerned, 'though it's not easy to judge in this lighting. Another time, soon, I hope. Now, can I run you home? My car's outside. Have you found somewhere, or are you in the nurses' block?'

She accepted the lift gratefully, and told him about Anne and the flat. When they arrived Fleur asked him in for coffee.

'Thanks, but no. You're pale. Go and eat something and then get straight to bed. Doctor's orders. I'll probably see you tomorrow, and then we'll fix a date.'

She waved as he drove away, then let herself into the block of flats. Anne was already there, and the delicious smells of hot soup and grilling lamb chops filled the small kitchen.

'Good. I was beginning to think I'd have to eat both chops,' Anne said, putting cutlery out. 'Were you kept late?'

'No, I had a drink with Steve. Anne, he was there, in the pub,' Fleur said as she hung up her jacket in the hall.

Anne stared at her in astonishment. She had no need to ask who Fleur meant. He had been a constantly recurring topic of conversation almost every day, however much Fleur protested that she wanted to forget all about it.

'Did he see you?' she asked now in practical tones.

'No. I was at the back, watching for Steve, and they only stayed a few minutes,' Fleur replied as she came into the kitchen. 'He was with a woman, all attentive,' she added.

Anne cast her a swift glance, but said nothing as she busied herself ladling out soup.

'I still don't understand what happened,' Fleur said after she had taken a few mouthfuls. 'Why didn't Sister Beasley report me? It must have seemed a marvellous opportunity for her.'

'She was off duty next day, and as you were leaving she might have realised it was pointless,' Anne suggested. 'When there are complaints the investigations take weeks while they interview everyone in sight to get at the truth.'

'They wouldn't have needed to, she and Liza saw it. And the next day hadn't been her day off, she changed it. And Liza was off too, which was odd as she'd only just come onto the ward.'

'At least no-one at the party seemed to know about it,' Anne reminded her.

'And that's another mystery. After all the rumours flying about I'd have expected it to be common knowledge by then. But no-one even mentioned it, not even in a sly, hinting way.'

'It was our leaving party, perhaps they all felt embarrassed, or wanted to be nice,' Anne suggested. 'Which reminds me, we ought to have a house warming here. We know enough people by now to fill the place. There's Dave and Steve, people from your ward and their boy friends, same for my course friends, and talking of handsome brutes, there's the fabulous Russell Delaney. If he'll come. I'm not surprised they all swoon when he only smiles at them. Is he good looking!'

'Where did you meet him?' Fleur asked, not interested in Anne's raptures about handsome men, but feeling that her friend was waiting for a response.

'He was operating this morning, gall stones, and we were observing. I know I'm only a raw beginner in Theatre, but he really is streets ahead of anyone else I've seen. So cool, and decisive, and he doesn't make sarcastic comments if the right implements aren't ready at exactly the moment he wants them. He gets much better co-operation that way, too,' she added. Anne had recently done a course in psychology, Fleur recalled, and she laughed, her mood suddenly lighter.

'I don't suppose he'd be interested in coming here,' she said warningly. 'Besides, David would be jealous.'

'Oh, we're not serious,' Anne said, a

little too airily, 'I was thinking he'd suit you better than Steve. He's much more exciting, I'm sure.'

'I've had enough excitement to last me a long time,' Fleur protested. 'The chops are burning.'

Anne leapt up with an exclamation of horror to rescue them, and then returned to her suggestion of a party. They checked their duties, for the next few weeks, agreed a date in early December, made some tentative lists, and then Fleur pleaded tiredness and retreated to bed.

But not to sleep. The sudden unexpected sight of him had made her restless, and her thoughts were busy with speculation about what he could be doing in London. Perhaps it wasn't so odd for him to be in the capital, but to be in exactly the same part of it where she was did seem strange.

She didn't even know his name, or what he did. Nor how he had come to be in St John's in the first place. Much as she insisted that she wanted only to forget him, she found that lack of knowledge intensely frustrating. Everything had happened so quickly that she had never seen his notes. When she had returned to duty the following day he had gone, and she had been so embarrassed she hadn't cared to question any other nurses.

Now she wished that she had, for at least that would tell her whether she was likely to encounter him again. The thought made her shiver apprehensively. It was not only the suddenness of what happened, but the strange effect it had had on her. No-one else had stirred her like that and Fleur, fundamentally honest, could not maintain the fiction that it was only surprise which had sent her blood surging about her veins, and her heart beating furiously. Her lips tingled still as she recalled the sensations of his mouth on hers, insistently persuading her to what she knew would soon have been an abject surrender.

Even though she was on a late duty the next day she was pale and tired, with dark smudges under her eyes from sleeplessness. Listlessly she counted sheets in the small cupboard near the entrance of the ward, and was emerging with a pile of them in her arms, stifling a yawn, when she became aware of several people entering the ward.

She stepped back to avoid a group of students accompanying a consultant on his ward round. She waited for them to go past, her eyes lowered, then almost dropped the sheets as her chin was grasped in a firm hand and her face tilted upwards.

'Are you burning the candle, or is it the air of London that has driven those delicious roses from your cheeks?' a deep, well-remembered voice asked, a hint of laughter in it.

Fleur's eyes flew upwards, and met smiling blue ones. She was of average height, and had not realised before just how tall he was. He had, after all, been sitting when she first saw him, and last night she had been too astonished to notice such details. Now her bemused gaze took in the white coat he wore, the stethoscope in his pocket, and then a wave of emotion stronger than anything else she had ever experienced swept over her, compounded of shame, fury, embarrassment, and an urgent need to remove herself at once from such close proximity.

'You!' she breathed, stepping back so that he had to release her chin. And then, although she was already sickeningly aware of the answer. 'What are you doing here?'

'Oh, I work here,' he said lightly. 'I've been waiting with some impatience to welcome you to Chad's, Staff Nurse Tremaine. You'll be a delightful recruit for us, competent and decorative. But I owe you an apology, which I couldn't offer you when last we met,' he went on, his eyes twinkling reprehensibly at the recollection of that meeting. 'I'll take you to dinner tonight and make amends properly.'

Before Fleur could reply, but whether she intended to refuse indignantly or berate him for his former behaviour, she could not afterwards recall, he had left her. He joined the others at the bed of a new patient, and she retreated further into the linen cupboard to hide her burning cheeks and angrily flashing eyes.

THREE

She contrived to keep out of the students' way and after they had gone concentrated on monitoring the progress of a patient newly returned from theatre. It was a busy day and Fleur forgot her tiredness, only realising it again when she and one of the other staff nurses went off for a meal late in the afternoon.

Jenny was small, plump, dark and placid. She had trained at Chad's, still lived in the hostel, and had been especially helpful to Fleur during her first few days. They shared a table with Sue and Angie from orthopaedics, both bright eyed with excitement.

'Have you heard?' Angie demanded and Jenny shook her head.

'Heard what? We're too busy to gossip, unlike you taking rest cures in orthopaedics,' she said teasingly.

Angie laughed. 'Russell Delaney is engaged at last,' she announced in an awed tone.

Jenny stared at her. 'I don't believe it! He's not the type to settle down, not the glamorous Russell.'

'Have you met him yet?' Sue asked Fleur.

'I've heard he's the hospital heart breaker,' she replied.

'And how!' Sue said in a grim tone. 'Be warned, stay away from him. He pays every pretty new nurse extravagant attentions, wining and dining her until she's dizzy, and then drops her flat, no explanation, nothing, always perfectly charming when

41

they meet but never a hint of another date!'

'Was that what happened to you?' Jenny asked sympathetically, 'Diane Meadows almost had a breakdown last year, and eventually left, she couldn't stand seeing him about all the time. But who on earth has snared him?'

'Mr Havelock's new secretary. Her name is Rowena Kingsley.'

Jenny whistled soundlessly. 'Related to the Monarch?'

'His daughter,' Sue nodded, and turned to Fleur. 'Mr Havelock's our most eminent brain surgeon, and Mr Kingsley, nick-named the Monarch, the equally distin-guished transplant man. Between them they practically run Chad's, and no senior appointments are made without their blessing.'

'And Russell is very ambitious,' Angie said dryly. 'How useful for him to have a friend in both courts, as it were!'

'She's very beautiful too,' Sue said consideringly. 'Tall, blonde, cool and elegant, just the sort of girl Russell prefers, and looking far too remote ever to have to be concerned with the mere task of earning a living.'

42

'Does she work for Mr Havelock in his Harley Street clinic?' Jenny asked, and Sue shook her head.

'No, just his two days here. Though she'd fit in with the decor there far better than at Chad's,' she added, looking round critically at the shabby pale green walls which badly needed repainting, and the ancient but sturdy canteen furniture. 'Come on, Angie, back to the grind, we haven't got all day to sit over our three course luncheon like some! See you.'

Jenny eyed her orange juice, salad and apple consideringly. She was trying to lose weight before all the Christmas festivities, she had told Fleur.

'I wonder if I could pretend it's caviar and pheasant and stilton?' she asked. 'How exciting. But avoid him, he's dangerous,' she added, quartering her tomato exactly.

'The notorious Russell Delaney? But surely, if he's engaged now he won't be flirting with other girls,' Fleur replied.

'No engagement will stop that man,' Jenny scoffed. 'And if it's all true she'll only be here a couple of days a week to keep an eye on him. Hello,' she added, as another nurse joined them, and promptly repeated the news.

43

This is how gossip spreads, Fleur thought despondently, imagining the staff at St John's repeating the rumours about herself and that dreadful man. He was actually a doctor at Chad's, she reminded herself, and shivered. She could not avoid him for ever, she would have to work with him, and be constantly reminded of what she so desperately wanted to forget. Russell Delaney couldn't be half as dangerous as he was, she thought, wishing that Jenny could talk of something else.

At last they left the canteen. As the time for finishing drew near, Fleur grew anxious. After issuing his surprising invitation—no, command, she corrected angrily—he had simply walked away. He had not waited for her to accept, or suggested a time. She hoped he wasn't serious, but nonetheless kept a wary eye open as, having handed over to the night staff, she went to change into her outdoor clothes.

Today she had a green and white checked skirt, white shirt and vee-necked green sweater, with the same boots and jacket. Pulling the jacket collar high about her face she went quickly to the main entrance, nearest the bus stop she used.

She had thought about leaving the

hospital by one of the other entrances, but it would have been inconvenient, cold and tiring to walk further than necessary to the next bus stop or the tube station. It would be silly to take precautions against nothing more than a casual remark.

Besides, she told herself firmly, even if the arrogant man did waylay her he couldn't force her to accept his invitation. He could scarcely abduct her in full view of the porter's lodge and all the people around.

He had been joking, she thought, when a quick glance round the entrance lobby failed to reveal him. She went hastily across to the huge old doorway. There were cars parked either side of the short drive, which was well lit, and she could see no-one waiting in any of them. She began to run as she saw her bus approaching along the road.

She was level with the last car when a man in a dark suit stepped from behind it and grasped her elbow, causing her to fall against him as her dash was abruptly halted.

'Good evening, Staff Nurse Tremaine,' a deep, somewhat mocking voice greeted her. 'You appear to be in a great hurry?'

Aware out of the corner of her eye that her bus was cruising blithely past the stop, Fleur ground her teeth in fury. She glared up into his handsome face, the features strongly defined, the blue eyes smiling down into hers.

'Now see what you've done!' she groaned. 'It's an hour before the next, even if it's on time, and it's freezing!'

He glanced at the now receding bus. 'But you don't need a bus. You're having dinner with me, or had you forgotten?'

'I am not!' Fleur retorted furiously. 'If you think I'm ready to drop everything and provide entertainment for you just because you order it, instead of asking me, you're very much mistaken. And let go of my arm, you're hurting me!'

He eyed her calmly, but dropped his hand obediently.

'I see, you're annoyed because I didn't wait for an answer,' he said, aggravatingly cool. 'I looked for you when we'd finished and you'd vanished. You could have refused me then.'

'I wish I had,' Fleur muttered, 'though you're quite capable of making a scene there if you think you're being thwarted!'

'How do you know so much about

me?' he asked, a gleam of amusement in his eyes.

'I don't even know your name, and I don't want to!' Fleur shot back at him. 'I do know that you're an arrogant, selfish brute, who caused a lot of trouble for me before and—'

'I want to apologise for that,' he interrupted swiftly. 'That's why I asked you out. Won't you permit me to make amends? And I'll drive you home now as I've caused you to miss your bus.'

'Never is convenient,' Fleur snapped. 'And I'm quite capable of making my own way home, thanks. Taxi!'

She turned to hail a taxi which had deposited a passenger at the hospital entrance and scrambled in, waiting until the door was firmly shut before giving her address to the driver.

She was still shaking when she reached home, but Anne was out and she had no-one to tell of her fury and indignation.

Suddenly exhausted, she forced herself to heat up some soup, then went to bed, to toss restlessly, and dream of the wretched man when she finally dropped into an uneasy sleep.

The next day, fortunately, she was off

duty, so was able to sleep late. When she found herself unable to concentrate on anything in the flat, her thoughts too preoccupied with her encounters with this man, whose name she still did not know, she determined to go shopping in an attempt to distract herself.

For warmth she wore a snug, close fitting dress made from a woollen mixture, cream flecked with brown, but when the biting wind whipped round her legs as she walked to the tube she promised herself that she would look for a long coat, since her jacket was not going to be warm enough this winter.

She explored the huge Oxford Street stores, lunched, and bought Christmas presents for her schoolboy brother and her parents. Then she turned her attention to clothes. With winter threatening she bought a heavy sweater, bright with a red and green pattern on a white background, cord jeans, and a long, woollen coat in a warm golden shade.

Laden with parcels, she let herself into the flat. As she was trying on the coat again, she heard Anne come in, and came out of her bedroom to greet her friend.

'I've been shopping,' she announced.

Anne looked briefly at the coat, smiled crookedly, then turned to hang up her own.

Fleur frowned. It was so unlike Anne not to be interested in clothes, her own or anyone else's.

'What is it? Are you ill? What's happened?' she demanded.

Anne sighed, and looked helplessly at Fleur.

'Let's eat first. Have we anything in the fridge?'

'The rest of that casserole, salad and cheese. Just a minute while I get rid of this, and it should be ready.'

She hung up her coat while in the kitchen Anne took the casserole out of the oven and helped herself to some, urging Fleur to do the same. Then she sat staring at it. Fleur, by now seriously alarmed, sat down opposite her.

'For Pete's sake tell me,' she begged. 'Is it David?'

Anne shook her head, sighed deeply, lifted a forkful of food to her mouth, looked at it as though she did not know what it was, and lowered it back onto her plate.

'I hate having to tell you, but it's

better that you're warned,' she said at last, slowly.

'Warned? What of?' Fleur demanded.

'It's all over the hospital that you got the sack for flirting with the patients,' she said baldly. 'The details are to do with that man, and they're pretty accurate.'

'But I didn't get the sack!' Fleur said, aghast.

'Things get distorted. You could have done, if you hadn't already been leaving.'

'It's him!' Fleur said slowly. 'I haven't had the chance to tell you yet, Anne, but he's a doctor, a surgeon, I think, at Chad's. That's why I saw him in the Crown.'

'Who? You don't mean—oh, no!'

'Yes. He was with some students yesterday morning, and recognised me. He told me—not asked—that he'd take me out to dinner last night, then walked away.'

'What happened?' Anne demanded.

'I was leaving last night, with no intention of going out with him. He stopped me just outside and we had a row. I missed the bus and grabbed a taxi. He must have spread the story about to get his revenge. Oh, I could wring his neck!'

She was still furiously angry the next

day, and the knowing looks from the other nurses did little to improve her mood. Deciding to tackle the problem directly, Fleur went for lunch with Jenny and demanded to be told what was being said. Jenny reluctantly confirmed that it was much as Anne had reported.

'But it's so stupid!' Fleur exclaimed. 'I'd never have been able to come to Chad's if that had been on my records, would I?'

'Then how did the rumour start?' she asked quietly.

'One of the sisters did report me, once. For being too friendly with male patients,' she added, and Jenny nodded.

'You're a very friendly person, Fleur, but no-one thinks anything of it on a woman's ward. They might if the patients were men, especially if someone was jealous of you.'

'She couldn't prove anything, and I didn't get a formal warning, but people believe there's no smoke without fire, so when—' she halted suddenly, then realised that she must tell the embarrassing truth to scotch the rumours. 'It was my last few days,' she went on. 'I was sent to a new patient, with suspected concussion, in a side ward. He was out of bed, trying to find his clothes, and when I tried to get him back into bed he pulled me down on top of him and kissed me.'

She shivered at the recollection, and Jenny exclaimed in sympathy and put her hand briefly on Fleur's.

'And someone made the wrong interpretation?'

Fleur nodded, then leaned closer across the table and spoke in as low a voice as she could.

'It's worse than that. Yes, Sister came in and found us struggling—I'd just slapped his face—and she sent me off duty. I thought I'd be hauled up to the SNO, but for some reason no more was said. I suppose she thought it wasn't worth the hassle as I was leaving the next day but I was surprised. Both she and the other nurse who was there loathed my guts. I'd have expected them to take any opportunity to harm me.'

'Then that's not too bad,' Jenny said comfortingly. 'People will soon forget, when there's another piece of gossip which amuses them, and there's nothing on record.'

'But that's not all. The man, I never did find out his name, works here. He's a surgeon, I think. He was doing the rounds the other day, and afterwards we had another row. He must have spread this story out of sheer vindictiveness, to get some kind of revenge. I'll never be allowed to forget it while he's here. I'll have to leave Chad's, and I was enjoying it so much!'

Jenny was staring at her in astonishment.

'What a dreadful coincidence. No wonder you're upset. Though perhaps not,' she said suddenly. 'A coincidence, I mean. I don't notice the Sports and Social Club much, but I heard one of the rugger team had been kept in for observation overnight after a match with one of the other hospitals. I forget where, but that could explain what he was doing at St John's. Anyway, surely we can turn this to your advantage. If we let people know it was because you rejected him, and that he's being spiteful because of that and spreading distorted stories about you, they'll laugh at him. They'll soon work out that you couldn't have got the sack, so although it'll be embarrassing for a while, he'll come out of it looking much more foolish.'

'I wish I could believe that,' Fleur said tensely.

'Of course you will,' Jenny said bracingly.

'First we must find out his name. Was he there today?'

'No, and I don't know the consultant he was with.'

'Well, describe him and I'll probably recognise him,' Jenny said soothingly. 'We suspect he plays rugger, and can check who's in the team. How old is he? Tall or short, dark or fair?'

'There's no need to,' Fleur said in a hollow voice. 'He's just come in, at the back of the queue, in a dark suit.'

Jenny turned round eagerly, then looked back at Fleur, her smile gone.

'It's no earthly use,' she said slowly. 'We can't say that, Fleur. No-one would ever believe that you rejected him. No-one has ever been known to, you see. That's Russell Delaney.'

FOUR

Fleur found it increasingly difficult to endure the whispers and speculative glances of the other staff. Some were amused at the story, others seemed sympathetic, and a few girls who cherished dreams of Russell Delaney directed their jealousy equally at Fleur and Rowena Kingsley. The rumours of the latter's engagement to the handsome surgeon added spice to what was a favourite topic of conversation for days.

No formal announcement had been made, and it was generally assumed that this was due to Rowena's father being on a two month lecture tour of Japan, Australia and New Zealand.

'They'll throw a big party to celebrate,' Jenny said one day. 'Have you seen her ring? She was wearing it yesterday.'

'A huge emerald, isn't it?' Anne asked. 'She was flashing it around yesterday when she was here. I must say I thought it a bit ostentatious. I'd prefer a more discreet one.'

'I don't suppose anyone else here could afford one like it,' Angie put in. 'Russell's family own some enormous business, a building firm, I think, he's always had pots of money. My cousin trained with him and even as a student, he had a Porsche.'

The four girls were in the bar of an West End theatre during the interval. As often happened, spare tickets were sent to the hospitals, and they had been able to get some. The play was dreary, although billed as one of the greatest comedies of all time, and events at Chad's were of far greater interest than the fortunes of the rather insipid characters on stage.

Fleur, though, wished they could talk of something else. She had seen Rowena's ring when the secretary had come to the ward with a message from Mr Havelock. Sister had been off duty and Fleur had been in charge. It was obvious from the somewhat sharp glance Rowena had given her when Fleur's name had been mentioned that she had heard all about the episode at St John's, and equally obvious that she did not like having to be polite.

'She's haughty and supercilious, gives orders, doesn't say thank you. I felt she was bursting to tear me apart,' Fleur said later to Anne. 'Her fingers were clenched, as if she could barely keep them off me. How she types with those talons, I don't know,' she added, with a critical look at her own short, neatly filed nails.

'Have you seen him again?' Anne asked.

'I've kept out of his way when he comes round the ward,' Fleur replied. 'And next week, thank goodness, I'm on nights, so I won't have to keep my eyes peeled for him. He doesn't use the canteen much, I've only seen him there once.'

Her first night on duty was uneventful, no emergencies, just the usual round of post operative observations and a couple of wakeful, talkative patients. She could relax from the fear of meeting Russell Delaney for the first time in a week or more, and felt unusually energetic, even at the end of her long hours.

It was a cold, sunny morning, with a touch of frost in the air when she came off duty, and after a cup of coffee with Anne, who had a late start that morning watching a session of micro-surgery, she decided to walk home.

'I'll get these things, they'll keep,' she said as she rose to leave the canteen, a list in her hand. They had been discussing their party, arranged for two weeks time.

'You can get the paper plates from that shop I found,' Anne reminded her. 'Can you carry all the tins?'

'If not I'll go out again this afternoon, when I've slept.'

She went out, swinging along with light, supple strides in the fresh morning air. The morning rush hour was over, and traffic was light.

She wore her new coat over a thick sweater and her brown skirt, and her hair swung in a loose golden curtain about her head. Relishing the crisp weather after days of damp miserable cold, she smiled as she walked along, staring with bright, eager eyes at the old buildings, pausing occasionally to read a blue plaque which told her who had lived there. She must buy a guide book and walk home more frequently. It would be good for her, and she could explore on the way.

She bought paper cups, plates and napkins, plastic cutlery, and, because she could not resist them, a set of mugs depicting scenes from London life. Most of their guests would have to make do with the paper cups for wine, but they would be able to serve coffee in these.

She was struggling to manage all her shopping, rather more bulky than she had intended, and fish in her bag for the key to the flat, when a familiar voice spoke just behind her.

'Can I help?' and before she could turn round Russell Delaney had deftly relieved her of several carrier bags.

'What are you doing here?' she demanded, when she had recovered her breath.

'Oh, I just happened to be passing,' he replied, 'and saw a damsel in distress. Weren't you looking for your key?'

Fleur looked down at her shoulder bag, for the moment uncomprehending, then glanced back at him suspiciously.

'Thank you, I can manage,' she said curtly, trying unsuccessfully to retrieve the shopping from his grasp.

'It would be simpler to open the door while I hold these,' he remarked, a gleam of amusement in his eyes. Then he glanced at the contents, and back at Fleur. 'A party?' he asked softly.

'Please give them back to me,' she replied sharply.

'There's no need to be afraid of me,' he said gently. 'I want to apologise. I must have been suffering from concussion, after all,' he added with a grin. 'Or delusions that I was in heaven and an angel was nursing me. Now, will you let me take you to dinner soon to make amends?'

Fleur gulped in amazement. How could he, so recently engaged, ask another girl for a date?

'I don't think that would stop the

rumours,' she snapped. 'Now go away, I can manage perfectly well by myself!'

'Rumours are usually inaccurate, so why be concerned? Why don't you open the door? Afraid I'll force my way in?' he asked, amused.

Fleur looked hastily away. That had been in her mind.

'I promise I won't,' he added, laughter in his voice, and she glanced quickly back at him, frowning in disbelief.

'I've little reason to trust you,' she said bitterly.

'Then you'll have to get to know me better,' he replied swiftly. 'A bargain. As you're too scared to trust yourself to my tender mercies I'll go straight away now on condition I'm invited to your party.'

Fleur was astounded, and before she could think of something scathing enough to say he smoothly deposited the shopping bags at her feet, gave her a mocking smile and walked away.

She stared after him, bemused, until she saw him open the door of a car some hundred yards away. Not a Porsche now, she noted absently, but although she could not recognise what else it was, it certainly was not a common make.

Then she began to wonder why he had been here. It was not the sort of street where he would have friends, and there were no shops nearby that might attract him. Also it was incredibly difficult to find a parking place, so how long had he been parked so suspiciously close to the flat?

She shrugged away the thought that he had discovered her address from the hospital records and come on purpose to waylay her. If he really wanted to speak to her he could do so at Chad's. Of course if would add to the rumours but he had started them in the first place, so presumably he had no conscience about what he had done, and no wish to hide anything from Rowena.

It must have been a coincidence. She would not believe anything else, she told herself firmly, and then turned to her door as he drove past, waving casually.

Why, she chided herself angrily as she fumbled again for her key, had she stared after him so stupidly? He would preen himself, thinking that she had been watching him, whereas she had been so bemused she had not been aware of what she was looking at.

Growing more and more angry with

herself she eventually controlled her trembling fingers and unlocked the door. She deposited the shopping in the kitchen, then stood staring at it, once more distracted. Why had he tried to make that ridiculous bargain with her? He wouldn't want to come to their party.

But what if he did, an insistent inner voice asked. Fleur shrugged. It was impossible. He meant to tease her, for some inexplicable reason. Besides, she thought hopefully, he had asked for no details and would not know when to come.

He knew where she lived, the inner voice reminded her. Once again she tried to ignore it, and when that failed, to explain away their meeting as pure coincidence.

She decided, after several hours of sleepless tossing, not to tell Anne. Her friend would be concerned and it was pointless for both of them to start worrying about whether Russell Delaney would gatecrash their party.

She hurriedly decided to invite two of the younger housemen, burly, rugger playing six footers, to the party. Russell was also a rugger player, she recalled, and more than six feet tall, then tried to persuade herself that since he had been injured he couldn't be very good. Two of them should be able to throw him out if he did gatecrash.

She shrugged away the thought that they might not relish ejecting their superior from a party, however private it was. Surely he would not come. But she would ask the others.

For some days she saw nothing of Russell. On nights, she was insulated from the hospital gossip, and the ward was peaceful until, around midnight on her last night, an emergency patient was admitted after an operation for burst appendix.

Fleur had just settled the patient, a woman in her mid-twenties, and was sitting beside her monitoring a faint and irregular pulse when she heard soft footsteps approaching.

'Go and have your break my sweet, I'll stay here. That pulse rate is worrying and I want to be sure she's OK.'

Fleur glanced up, startled, and just prevented herself from making some angry comment. Russell, his eyes looking tired, was smiling down at her.

She stood abruptly, but careful not to disturb the other patients, some of whom had wakened when the new patient had been wheeled in, and who were just dropping off to sleep again.

'Go and eat, then I'd appreciate a cup of coffee.'

Fleur swallowed. He was on duty, and she could scarcely refuse that, or disobey him. Besides, she needed to get away from the turmoil his sudden appearance, and the endearment he had so reprehensibly used, had caused in her body.

She was trembling, her own pulse rate distinctly raised. Not surprising, perhaps, for his soft approach had startled her.

She had a few quiet words with the other staff nurse, answered an eager query from the student, anxious to learn all she could of the various abdominal operations she was seeing, and went to the canteen. She forced herself to eat some sausages and chips, the only meal the night staff seemed able to produce, and had just pushed away the plate, half full, when Steve came in. He crossed to her table, smiled wearily and sat down.

'That was a near one,' he commented. 'Another half an hour and even Russell wouldn't have been able to save her.'

'You've been in theatre? You mean the

appendicectomy?'

'Yes. She's on your ward, isn't she? Russell said he'd check on her, she lost a huge amount of blood in theatre. I think he intends to stay all night unless another emergency comes in, he's worried she might relapse. Lord knows how he does it, I can't. I need cat naps on night call, and this is my first night on. Russell was called out twice last night, a kid with something he'd swallowed piercing his stomach wall, then two drunken idiots who'd smashed up their motor bike as well as themselves. And I know he had a full list today.'

'He's up there now, no doubt waiting for his cup of coffee,' Fleur said, with a sudden keen desire to rush back to the ward. He'd need that coffee, she was thinking. No wonder he looked exhausted if this was his second night without sleep.

A vivid picture suddenly came to her mind, one she had unsuccessfully tried to banish on many previous occasions, of him sitting on that hospital bed, his tanned, naked back towards her. Now there was an addition to that picture, of herself on the bed beside him, smoothing the tiredness out of him with gentle massage of his broad shoulders and strong neck muscles.

'I ought to go back,' she said hurriedly, hoping that her unruly thoughts did not show in her face.

'Wait a moment. I've seen so little of you. Will you come out to dinner with me when you're off nights?'

'I'd love to. Thanks, Steve. It's my last duty tonight.'

'Then how about Saturday, it will give you a couple of days to recover. I'll pick you up at seven, OK?'

'Fine. I must go now, though.'

Russell was standing beside the bed, carefully adjusting the intravenous infusion. She went softly into the small kitchen and switched on the kettle, found a jug and spooned coffee into it.

She had just poured on the water when a slight sound made her look up. He was leaning against the kitchen doorway.

'How is she?'

'I think she'll be OK. It was touch and go, and she'll need watching for a day or so.'

'Shall I go and sit by her?' Fleur asked quickly. 'The coffee will be ready in a few moments.'

'Then you can have some too. Your

student is on watch. She seems a bright kid, reliable and anxious to learn, asking questions. She'll call if there's any change.'

As she did not move, he stepped across the tiny kitchen, picked up the jug, and poured two cups of coffee. Then as he turned to reach for the door of the fridge his arm brushed against Fleur's breast, and she felt as though she had been electrocuted, so intense was the shock which went through her.

He did not seem to notice the contact, or her instinctive step backwards, but took a bottle of milk from the fridge, poured some into the saucepan and set it on the hotplate.

'I'm sorry, I thought you'd prefer it black,' Fleur stammered in some confusion.

'Only after a good meal,' he explained, 'and I don't seem to have eaten for days. Are there any biscuits? I recall that Sister Reynolds usually keeps a good supply.'

He was investigating a couple of tins as he spoke, and his eyebrows shot up in surprise.

'What have we here? Brandy snaps? And home made, I'll swear. I haven't seen anything looking so good for years. Do you think I dare help myself?'

'Of—of course,' Fleur said, confused once again.

The rich gingery scent mingled with the aroma of the coffee. Fleur turned away to watch the milk, adding it to both cups.

'Mm, delicious. Where on earth did Sister find them? Won't you have one? There won't be any left for you soon.'

'I—I made them, I like them, especially on nights,' Fleur said slowly. 'Please, have as many as you wish.'

He took another, nodding approval. 'Is this your one speciality, or do you cook everything so deliciously?'

'I enjoy cooking,' Fleur said defensively, suspecting that he was laughing at her.

He grinned, and shut the tin. 'A woman of many talents. Perhaps instead of taking you out to dinner I ought to be encouraging you to cook one. Much more intimate than a crowded restaurant, however discreetly separated the tables are.'

Fleur frowned and shook her head. 'I'm not coming out with you.'

'Why not?'

'Why not?' she repeated, stupified. How could he possibly try to date another girl after getting engaged to Rowena.

'That's what I said. What's to stop me from taking you out, especially as I still haven't apologised adequately?'

Fleur took a deep breath. 'I don't appreciate being the butt of sly jokes,' she said bitingly. 'It was bad enough finding out that you worked at Chad's, and having to meet you on the wards, without everyone else sniggering about what you...what happened, watching to see what other tricks you had planned for me! And I don't two-time anyone, whatever you do! You behaved despicably then, you could have got me the sack and ruined my career, and you're doing your best to wreck my life here as well, when all I want to do is forget that I ever saw you!'

He was staring at her in amazement, his eyes narrowed to thin slits, a white line of fury about his lips.

'You vicious little prude!' he ejaculated. 'One kiss, which I admit should not have happened, but which was far too tempting to refuse, and you make all this fuss! Anyone would think I'd raped you at the very least! Where the devil did you get your reputation, Nurse Flirt?'

With that, before Fleur realised his attention or could move to avoid him, he stepped towards her where she stood at the far end of the narrow, tiny kitchen.

Seizing her hands, which she had instinctively raised in front of her, he pulled them behind her and grasped both in one of his own iron-strong hands, while the other forced her head round as she tried desperately to evade him, and his lips, hard, warm, and insistent, came down on hers.

Pinned against the cupboards behind her, Fleur had no chance of avoiding him, and her senses reeled as once more she felt that hard, muscular body against her own. Sensations she had been trying desperately and ineffectually to erase from her mind swept back in even greater force, and she was unaware of everything except the need to remain unresponsive.

Summoning all her willpower she somehow stayed passive, preventing her body from reacting to the strange and potent forces he was releasing in her. Instinctively she knew that if she once permitted him to realise the effect he had on her, she would be totally lost.

The battle was almost more than she could bear. His lips grew soft and gently explored hers, which quivered with the effort not to merge in to his. A gentle finger stroked the curve of her cheek, down across her firm little chin, and then travelled unbearably slowly along her throat until reluctantly, it seemed, it stopped at the collar of her uniform.

Suppressing a moan of agony, Fleur began to struggle even more urgently, and suddenly found herself released. Leaning back she slowly drew her hand across her lips, her eyes huge and distressed as she stared speechlessly at him.

'I'll go and check another patient, then I'll be back to see this one, Staff Nurse Tremaine,' he said in a harsh voice, and turned abruptly to leave the kitchen.

Fleur breathed deeply, closed her eyes, but when the only result of that was to renew the sensations she had just experienced, she hurriedly opened them again. Shatteringly aware of the tremendous struggle it had been not to let him see how much she had wanted to forget everything and melt into his embrace, she stared unheedingly at the two untouched cups and breathed the lingering elusive fragrance of after shave mingled with brandy snaps and coffee.

FIVE

Somehow Fleur got through the rest of her duty, but later could recall only a few blurred impressions.

Russell had returned, hollow-eyed, unspeaking, and visited his patient briefly. He reappeared at frequent intervals, checking on her progress, and when he spoke to Fleur to order an increase in the amount of pethedine to be administered, he did so in a cold, even tone, not looking at her.

The patient was drowsy, but after a few hours all the indications were that she would recover without any additional problems, and Fleur, having settled her for what remained of the night, went mechanically about her other duties until able to escape, with immense relief, when she handed over to Sister.

She lay for a long time in the bath to try and relax, but although it was deep and hot she shivered at the memory of that shattering, devastating embrace.

'He's a fiend!' she said later to Anne,

as they ate supper from trays in the sitting room. She had not described the kiss or her own shameful reactions, but when Anne had returned home after her own day at the hospital and discovered her, pale and with a raging headache, Fleur had to say something.

'I wonder if Rowena knows about his wandering eye?' Anne speculated. 'It's too much, to get engaged to one girl and then start harassing another for dates! Though Rowena is rather cold—I've spoken to her several times about patients and she doesn't seem interested. It's a temporary part time job here while Mr Havelock's secretary is on maternity leave. She's got a share in a beauty salon or something. That's far more her line.'

'I don't want to leave Chad's,' Fleur said slowly, 'but I can't endure this much longer. First he spreads that story, then believes that stupid nick-name, and thinks he can treat me as contemptuously as he likes.'

'You mustn't think of leaving,' Anne said firmly. 'We'll stop him even if we have to complain to Rowena's father.'

'We can't for a couple of months,' Fleur said. 'Besides, I don't like involving other people, it's my problem.'

'We could threaten to, though,' Anne said musingly. 'An official complaint of unprofessional conduct wouldn't look very good on Mr Romeo Delaney's record, and might damage his prospects in the same way as he's trying to damage yours!'

'He either wouldn't care, or his word would be believed against mine,' Fleur said dejectedly.

'Still, it's worth a try,' Anne urged. 'Next time he tries to kiss you, tell him you'll make a complaint.'

'And if I'm forced to do it the rumours and talk would be worse,' Fleur replied, and Anne had no comfort to offer for she knew that Fleur was right. They might cause trouble for Russell Delaney, but Fleur would also suffer.

Silently determining to make some effort on her own initiative, Anne began to talk about the party, and then, worried at the drawn look on Fleur's face she persuaded her, much against her inclination, to take a sleeping pill.

'You need to sleep as much as the patients!' she insisted as Fleur wearily shook her head. 'I know we both hate unnecessary medication, but if you don't sleep you'll be unfit for anything. It's bad enough adjusting from nights to days without other complications making it impossible for you to rest. Just one Temazepam, please?'

More to stop her than because she thought it would do any good, Fleur agreed, and to her surprise she did enjoy a deep, dreamless sleep, awaking bodily refreshed but still with a cloud of gloom oppressing her spirits.

'Is it tonight you're going out with Steve?' Anne asked as they sat at breakfast.

'Heavens, I'd forgotten that. I'd better wash my hair. What are you planning?'

'To get more things for the party. David's bringing his car round later so that I can get the beer and wine. Come with us?'

'I don't think so, but is there anything I can get locally? It's too early to do any cooking, isn't it?'

'Mrs Wilson in the flat downstairs offered to let us use her freezer, so I'll make quiches and pizzas today. Could you mix the dough and bake the pastry cases? You're much better at it, and I'll do all the fillings after shopping.'

'Right. Bring David back to lunch, I'll

make a pie since we're doing pastry,' Fleur suggested.

She spent the morning cooking, and at lunch realised that David and Anne were clearly the best of friends. And more, she concluded, seeing the look in David's eyes as he watched Anne.

She was happy for Anne. David was a pleasant, equable man, open and uncomplicated. Not like Russell, she thought, and pulled herself up short. What on earth was she doing, even thinking of them together. It seemed highly probable that Anne would marry David, but there was no possibility that she and Russell Delaney would marry. She had no intention of even going out with him, apart from the fact that he was already engaged, she told herself in confusion, and wondered why the thought should cast her into deep depression.

'I'll see you at seven, if you're ready on time for once,' David said teasingly to Anne when he left, and she laughed.

'You're more likely to be late. I'll pay for dinner if I'm later than you! Now go, I've work to do, I can't spend Saturday afternoons lazing in front of the box like some people!'

She began on the food for the party,

chatting happily to Fleur, who was washing her hair and then inspecting her wardrobe in order to find something suitable to wear that evening.

At last she chose a boldly patterned black and white dress with plunging neckline.

'I need cheering up,' she explained as she sat in the kitchen stitching up the hem. 'I don't go in for bright reds and pinks, but I need to make a splash. There, is that level?' she asked, slipping off the pale blue housecoat she was wearing and pulling the dress over her head.

Anne regarded her thoughtfully. The large pattern had been cleverly placed to emphasise all the right curves, she realised, and the neckline, though deep, was tantalising rather than revealing. Fleur looked stunning.

Steve clearly agreed when he arrived, and seemed barely able to take his eyes from her. Anne and David had left, and as Steve helped Fleur on with her coat he bent to kiss her neck.

She swung round, startled. He had never before kissed her except briefly at the end of an evening. She had thought of him just as a good companion, easy and undemanding. Now all that was changed.

Perhaps the dress had been a mistake. She could not cope with two amorous surgeons, she thought in a panic.

'Let's go,' she said hurriedly, and thought that Steve followed her with considerable reluctance from the flat.

He took her to a small but expensive French restaurant close to the hospital.

'It's a favourite with the doctors,' he told her as they sipped sherry and read the excellent menu. 'Several of them have recommended it to me, though I've only been here once before.'

She was idly wondering who had been his companion on that occasion when two more of the medical staff at Chad's arrived and joined them as they waited for their tables. One was with his wife, a former nurse, the other with a girl who was a solicitor.

'Nothing to do with medicine, though I'm rapidly learning a great deal about it,' she said wryly when she had been introduced to Fleur and Steve. 'You people do tend to stick together.'

'It's the hours,' the other woman said. 'A wife who didn't understand could be really suspicious when her husband didn't turn up until hours after he'd promised.'

'Yes, an emergency's an excellent excuse,' her husband commented, 'and one can't ring home from the theatre to warn you to hold dinner. I wonder why anyone ever marries a doctor!'

'So do I,' she teased, and then Steve and Fleur were called to their table and saw no more of them.

To Fleur's relief they saw Anne and David letting themselves in as they arrived back at the flat. Steve had been uncharacteristically silent, and Fleur suspected that he would want to come in. However he refused coffee, saying that he had better go home as he was on duty the following morning.

From the way he held her hand and put his arm about her shoulders she knew that his feelings for her had changed into something warmer. She was not ready for it, and dreaded having to try and explain the reasons to him.

She had to exercise great control when he kissed her lingeringly outside the door of the flat. Her mind was protesting, and she had immense difficulty in preventing herself from shrinking away from the touch of his lips. This was not in the least like the effect Russell had on her, she thought involuntarily, recalling the burning desire which had swept over her when the other man had merely touched her accidentally.

Confused, ashamed of such recollections, she broke away, thanked him and let herself into the flat.

'I'll see you at Chad's next week, darling,' he replied lightly, apparently unaware of her turmoil.

She went straight to bed, but was unable to sleep for hours. How wretchedly complicated life was, she raged impotently. When a two-timing, untrustworthy rogue forced kisses on her, she had to exert tremendous efforts to stop herself from responding, yet when a decent, kind, thoroughly nice man like Steve wanted to kiss her she shrank away, hating it.

And hated his endearment, she realised with a shock. Many people used the term 'darling' lightly, but for Steve it was not a casual word. And she did not like the implications. She was not ready to commit herself to anyone.

Perhaps the shock of Russell's kisses made her unable to tolerate Steve's. That would make sense, and not imply she liked Steve less than Russell. She hated

Russell, she had not a single shred of liking for him.

What about the longing when she had found it so difficult not to respond, her inner voice tormented her. Chemistry, bodily sexual chemistry, she insisted, which was haphazard, but unnecessary. If only Steve elicited that response.

Angry at the direction of her errant thoughts she gave up all attempts to sleep, switched on the bedside light and tried to forget her problems by re-reading one of her favourite books. It was only partly successful, for she found her thoughts persistently intervening, but at last she fell into an uneasy doze, awaking to wonder bemusedly why the light was still on.

Her friends were overflowing with more gossip when she returned to work a few days later.

'Rowena has broken her engagement,' Jenny told her as they were setting up dressings trolleys. 'I heard yesterday, from a girl in theatre. It's stunned everyone, for after the triumph of capturing the man it's amazing to throw him over.'

Biting back the comment that Rowena was well rid of him, Fleur merely raised her eyebrows. Jenny was eager to go on.

'She wasn't wearing her ring on Friday, and was dreadfully pale and quiet. Someone saw Russell talking to her in the corridor, and she positively shouted at him and flounced off. He looked daggers when he realised that they'd been seen.'

'What caused it?' Fleur asked.

'Neither of them have breathed a word. But later the same day she walked straight past him without speaking. Perhaps we'll hear more when we go for lunch.'

However Fleur was delayed, helping to admit a new patient with a hiatus hernia, and went down to the canteen later than normal. Jenny had gone, and the canteen was crowded, but she found a small corner table. She propped a book in front of her, and jumped with startled dismay when she was spoken to.

'May I sit here?' Before she could reply Russell had pulled out the other chair and seated himself. He had just a cup of coffee, and he leaned back, regarding her with sombre eyes.

His chair was at an angle and blocked her only way out, Fleur realised in fury, her heart pounding with mingled astonishment and annoyance.

'I must go, I'm late back,' she stammered.

'I saw you come in not five minutes ago, when I was having my own lunch. Please listen. I want to apologise again. What I did was unpardonable, but whenever I see you I want to kiss you! Now I know that won't encourage you to come out with me, and I don't blame you, but will you at least let me buy you a drink tonight? We can go to the Crown, I won't drive you home, and I'll invite others too, for your protection!' he added, his eyes suddenly laughing at her.

He really did have almost hypnotic eyes, Fleur was thinking, and then looked up with a start as another man approached.

'Darling,' Steve greeted her, and she knew with utter certainty that if she had not been trapped in the corner out of reach he would have dropped a kiss on top of her head.

She fumed inwardly, unaware of why she was so angry, but faintly realising that she was unwilling to be identified as Steve's property.

He pulled another chair up, nodded to Russell, and unloaded the contents of his tray. Russell glanced from under suddenly lowered eyelashes from one to the other, then as Fleur did not speak he began to tell

Steve of an interesting article on relaxant drugs that he had read that morning.

'I must go back, we're busy,' Fleur said hastily, and this time Russell moved promptly for her to squeeze past.

'I'll pick you up at five,' Steve said to her, and she resented his air of ownership. She would need to stop it quickly she decided, and smiled at him.

'Sorry, Steve, I've made other arrangements,' she said briskly, and before he could protest walked swiftly towards the door.

'Attagirl,' Russell said softly as the doors swung to behind her. Fleur turned, startled, unaware that he had followed her.

'I didn't mean that I was coming out with you!' she exclaimed in dismay, but he didn't seem to hear her.

'I can't stand possessive people taking one for granted' he was saying. 'I'll see you in the Crown.'

With that he grinned and strode away. Fleur fumed. Talk about pots and kettles, she muttered, and then had to skip nimbly out of the way of a trolley one of the porters was pushing.

She spent most of the afternoon telling herself that she would not go. It was preposterous. If she did he would preen himself over another conquest. He was no longer engaged, perhaps using her to recapture Rowena's interest. Hastily she switched her thoughts to Steve. He needed to be taught a lesson, yet unless Steve actually saw her with Russell he would not receive it. Then she recalled the efficient grapevine in the hospital. Steve would know within minutes of entering Chad's the next day. And so would Rowena.

The thought of the gossip and speculation, the fuel it would add to the rumours about her own previous encounter with Russell made her determined not to give way, and even as she approached the bus stop she had no intention of entering the Crown. She could not afterwards recall the exact reasons why her feet had carried her round the corner and through the huge doors to be met by Russell inside the plush, warm saloon bar.

'I've bought you a martini,' he said, taking her arm to guide her to one of the secluded bays.

How could he be so obnoxiously sure she would come, she thought angrily, but could find nothing suitable to say in reply, since she had come, unaccountable though she found her actions.

Shivering, for even through her thick coat Fleur could feel his strong, slim fingers on her arm, she slid along the bench. Although he sat beside her he kept a distance away, and she was grateful that he appeared to have no intention of casually sliding his arm along the back of the bench. No, he was more direct than that, he'd take what he wanted without subterfuge, her inner voice warned sarcastically, but Fleur paid little heed.

'I've told you the effect you have on me,' he was saying in a cool, clinically detached voice, immediately proving her thoughts. 'Good subject for a research study, perhaps, but I doubt if we could find anyone sufficiently detached to undertake it. Is that the reason for your nickname?'

'The other students found it funny, my name and the fact that one of my first patients, when he got delirious, kept raving that he was going to marry me,' Fleur explained shortly.

'I can't imagine he was completely out of his mind, and he won't have been the only one with such ideas,' he added.

'Susceptible male patients always imagine themselves in love with their nurses. It's one of the hazards of the profession. Doctors have to put up with it too.'

'It's one of the advantages of being a surgeon. At least for some of the time the patients are out of action and one can feel safe,' he commented, and Fleur chuckled, relaxing herself. 'How long will you stay at Chad's? Do you want to specialise?'

From hospital topics their talk spread to other matters, and Fleur was soon telling him about her home.

'I miss the hills,' she confessed. 'We're very close to the Welsh border, only a short distance from Shrewsbury.'

'My parents have a cottage in that part of Wales,' he said. 'I loved holidays as a child, exploring castles, imagining myself a Welsh prince fighting English invaders. Sometimes I'd be a captured soldier escaping, or a spy behind enemy lines. Did you have such fantasies?'

'Sometimes, but I loved dogs and ponies. I wanted to be a vet, then decided I would be happier nursing people.'

'Didn't you want to be a doctor?' he asked curiously. 'Nursing is often second best with some people.'

'Only for a very short while. I doubt if

I'd have been accepted at medical school with my 'A' levels, and I wanted to be more closely involved with every aspect of caring for people. Nursing offered more variety, it's much better for me.'

They talked eagerly and Fleur lost track of the time. When they rose to leave and Russell escorted her to his car it seemed so natural to get in that afterwards Fleur could never explain why she had. Nor that fact that she made no demur when he drove to a small riverside restaurant, casually remarking that it was far enough from Chad's to be sure of not meeting other medics.

It was only much later when, without making the slightest effort to touch her hand, let alone kiss her, he drove her home, that she properly realised what had happened.

Entirely without meaning to she had done exactly as he had wished, spent the whole evening in his company, had dinner with him, and been thoroughly absorbed and happy the entire time. Not once, after the first few minutes, had she felt threatened, or even remotely uncomfortable. It had seemed so natural to be together, talking and eating and drinking, swapping reminiscences of childhood, all with a great deal of laughter, that she felt suspended in a dream. A dream that could not last.

SIX

Fleur saw Russell only briefly for several days, on ward rounds or when he came to see his own patients, and she had great difficulty persuading herself they really had spent the evening together. She felt as if she had been enchanted, in both senses. He had proved an entirely different kind of man to the one she had thought she knew, considerate, interesting, and devastatingly attractive. A man she could very easily fall in love with, she admitted honestly to herself, even without that electric current which ran between them every time he kissed her. Somehow he had bewitched her, inducing her to go with him, forgetting entirely the suspicions and fears she harboured.

But he had spread the story of her discomfiture, she recalled, hardening her heart against him. Any man who could do that should not be trusted, however adept he was at beguiling gullible nurses.

It was difficult to maintain her attitude when she was longing to see him again, and as she had carefully refrained from telling Anne, who had been out that night with David and not noticed her absence, she had no-one to confide in.

'Rowena's looking as black as thunder,' Jenny said one day.

'You seem to relish all the murky details,' Angie said with a laugh. 'What is it to you whether they're having a row?'

Jenny gave a rueful grin. 'I'm not sure,' she admitted. 'Partly I'm glad to see things going less than smoothly for the heart-throb of Chad's, and partly I'm fascinated that anyone could reject him.'

'He doesn't seem to be especially upset,' Angie remarked.

'Have you seen him?' Fleur could not resist asking.

'Only briefly, yesterday. He mentioned he'd be away most of the week, and Mr Markham was looking after his cases.'

Steve spoke once to Fleur, looking both hurt and puzzled, but apart from saying that he looked forward to the party on Saturday he made no attempt to arrange another date with her.

She was relieved, but guilty. Yet she had no cause to be for she had given him no encouragement, and the change in their relationship was all on his side. Or had been. He had been punctiliously polite, but his eyes were cold and he seemed withdrawn. She ought to be glad that he had taken the rebuff she had dealt him in such a way, for she could not feel towards him as he had seemed to wish.

Nor to anyone except Russell Delaney, she realised, and hastily suppressed the thought. Perhaps he had felt genuine remorse and that evening had been just an apology. After all, despite his broken engagement she could not expect him to fall in love with her. He had not suggested they meet again. How could he possibly turn to her after the gorgeous Rowena? He must be hoping the broken engagement would be resumed. His date with her had all too probably been made with that in mind.

Confused, miserable, Fleur could summon up little enthusiasm for the party. She and

Anne had Friday off, and spent the day making preparations and doing last minute shopping.

On Saturday they washed salad greens, mixed a variety of salads, cooked rice, defrosted the quiches and pizzas from Mrs Wilson's freezer, and were feeling worn out by mid afternoon.

'There's only salad dressings, bread and cheese to lay out, and mince pies to heat,' Anne said as they flopped in front of the electric fire with mugs of steaming coffee. 'Do you think we've got enough milk? Shall I fetch more cream?'

'No,' Fleur replied firmly. 'If we're short of anything now it's too bad. Do you want the bath first, or shall I?'

'You go, I'm too tired. Wake me up when you've finished.'

Fleur laughed, but half an hour later, refreshed and glowing from her tub, she found Anne curled up, fast asleep, on a cushion on the floor, her still full coffee mug beside her. She responded reluctantly to Fleur's admonitions, but an hour or so later was again her normal self, flying about the flat with small bowls of nuts and crisps, opening bottles, busy slicing long French rolls and placing baskets of them beside the cheeseboard, while Fleur dealt with the salads in the kitchen.

Fleur had treated herself to a stunning new dress. A deep hyacinth blue shot through with gold thread, it fell loosely from narrow shoulder straps to be caught in at her tiny waist by a belt of gold chains. Then the drapes hugged her slender hips and hinted at her long, shapely legs.

Anne, vivid and dark, had a plain tunic style dress in brilliant white, slit at the sides and with embroidered black and silver edging. They were putting the finishing touches to their make up when the first guests arrived.

'This is a fabulous party!' Jenny shouted an hour later, and from the noise the guests were making they seemed to agree. Steve had arrived early and busied himself with the bottles, which Fleur found both a help and a threat.

'He's acting the host,' she said to Anne in the kitchen. 'David has more right to do that, yet he's not being nearly so...obvious. Several people have given Steve funny looks.'

'Don't you want him to act as host?' Anne said curiously, and Fleur recalled that Anne was unaware of the complications that had arisen since her last date with Steve.

'It's taking too much for granted, I suppose.'

'Shall I see if I can get someone else to take over tactfully,' Anne suggested, and Fleur belatedly realised that such a move would release Steve to pay attentions to her, and she wanted that even less than what he was doing now.

'No, leave it, I'm being too sensitive,' she replied. 'Oh, there's the doorbell, I'll go. I thought everyone had come.'

'There's a few who said they might not be able to make it,' Anne said. 'Here, take this tray of mince pies, someone in the hall will open the front door.'

Fleur nodded and took the tray to the sitting room. She moved around checking that everyone had food and drink, encouraged a rather shy girl to talk to another, and then Steve called to her that they needed more ice.

'Have we plenty?' he asked, and she bit her lip to prevent a sharp retort at the proprietory 'we'.

'I'll get some,' she replied quietly, going to the kitchen.

By then several guests had migrated

there, and she had to squeeze her way past to the fridge. Angie stopped her to introduce her boyfriend, a large blond policeman, and when Fleur turned round again she came suddenly face to face with Russell, in jeans and a grey silk sweater, leaning negligently against the sink.

'How—how did you get in?' she asked blankly.

'Your friend Jenny opened the door to me,' he replied grinning at her confusion.

'But I didn't think you were coming!'

'Fleur, where's that ice?' Steve called, and she turned distractedly to see him waving the empty ice bucket.

'C—coming,' she stammered, and thankfully opened the fridge and hoped that her burning cheeks would be cooled by it.

She was fumbling with the ice-bags when Russell calmly took them from her and began to fill a bowl on the drainer.

'Angie, be a love and take these to Steve,' he asked a minute later and Angie, accustomed to instant obedience, did so though looking rather bewildered.

'We made a bargain, remember?' Russell said softly to Fleur.

Apart from being startled by his sudden

arrival, she had not expected to see him. She had almost forgotten the possibility his words had opened up.

'But you didn't know when it was,' she said.

'It wasn't difficult to discover,' he said. 'I was hurt not to receive an official written invitation, though.'

Fleur stared at him, speechless.

'I never thought you'd want to come,' she said at last.

'Why not, after you'd forgiven me my crass behaviour? I thought we were getting on famously, and had made a new start.'

'Come and meet Anne,' Fleur said desperately.

'I didn't come here to meet Anne, or anyone else,' he replied, a disturbing gleam in his eyes, 'but if you think I ought to demonstrate that I can be the perfect guest, even though an uninvited one, I'll come and behave properly.'

'I'm sorry, I didn't mean to be rude, I was startled,' Fleur apologised, flustered, as he tucked her arm through his.

'You look more than ever beautiful tonight,' he said softly as they went to the sitting room.

Fleur's colour rose again, and she was

aware of curious glances from hospital staff. Anne, even more startled than Fleur had been, recovered her wits and waved at the food.

'Help yourself, the bar's over there. We didn't start eating long ago, and I think there's plenty left.'

'What would you like to drink?' David asked, anxious to be helpful, and only just preventing himself from adding 'Sir'.

'White wine, please. Did you cook all the food?' Russell asked Anne politely, helping himself to a slice of pizza. 'Mm, delicious. I'll take some more while it's there. When people realise how good it is they'll be fighting for it.'

'Fleur made it,' Anne told him, and he turned to where Fleur was standing beside him, as though rooted to the spot.

'Even better than brandy snaps,' he said calmly, and she flushed to the roots of her hair as she recalled what had happened on that particular occasion.

'I must get some more ice,' she said, her voice strangled, and almost ran back to the kitchen. When she returned he was talking to the very pair of rugger players she had intended to use as throwers out, and she began to think he had an uncanny knack of reading her mind and a talent for spiking her guns.

For some time she managed to avoid him, but she could not escape the curious looks, and the heads close together as people speculated on Russell's latest conquest.

'I didn't know you were inviting Delaney,' Steve said rather peevishly, having relinquished control of the bar to David.

'I didn't know he was coming,' she replied. 'I invited him casually, when I couldn't very well avoid it,' she invented, 'and as he said nothing I thought he'd forgotten it.'

'He's causing gossip about you, and I don't like that,' Steve said censoriously.

'Neither would I like it if it were true, but surely his coming to our party isn't worth all this fuss,' Fleur retorted, forgetting that she had been perturbed and angry about the very same thing. 'They'll soon find something else to gossip about,' she added, trying to pacify him and convince herself at the same time, but ruefully aware that she had succeeded in neither aim when Steve pursed up his lips and shook his head, then walked slowly away from her.

She saw him coming back later, when people started to dance, but before he could reach her Fleur felt a strong arm about her waist and found herself clasped tightly in Russell's arms.

'I can't think why people prefer the kind of dancing where you lose your partner in the crowd,' he murmured. 'I choose to be as close to mine as possible when they're as delectable as you. Relax sweetheart, you trust me now, remember?'

'Perhaps I would if you didn't make that kind of remark,' Fleur replied tartly.

'Not even when it's true? You are delectable, and you can trust me, except when I've got concussion,' he added, and Fleur laughed, for the first time amused at the thought of their first meeting. Then she recalled that he had told others at Chad's of it, and her laughter stopped abruptly.

As if sensing her withdrawal he said no more, and they drifted sensuously in time to the soft romantic music. Fleur was acutely conscious of his nearness, the elusive tang of his aftershave, and his cheek resting lightly against her hair. He held her closely, but not excessively so, and when the music changed to a vibrant rock number he released her.

'Let's find another drink,' he suggested, taking her hand and leading her through the crush of people.

Steve had retreated to the bar and eyed them morosely. Russell found two plastic cups, filled them with wine, then steered Fleur towards a corner of the room where piles of cushions had been tossed on the floor.

She sank down on them, and he joined her, carefully balancing the wine.

'To you,' he murmured, handing her one of the cups. Before she could reply he began talking again about Chad's. 'Are you free at Christmas this year?' he asked after a while.

Fleur shook her hand. 'No, but I have the New Year. It's difficult to realise that Christmas is so close. I've only bought half my presents so far.'

'Will you go home?'

'Yes. I don't see my family very often, and like to spend holidays with them. My brother will still be on his school holidays, so my father is taking time off too. If I had more than a few days we might have gone skiing. What about you?'

'I'm on duty at Christmas, but as my parents are abroad I shall spend the New

Year with the Kingsleys.'

Fleur gasped, and was thankful for the dim lighting and that this corner was in a deep shadow. How could he refer to this so calmly, after the compliments he had been paying her?

The engagement must be on again, she thought, and felt her stomach lurch. Why was he pursuing her so obviously while committed to another woman? Were his habits of dalliance so deeply engrained that he could not stop?

She gulped the rest of her wine, and began to rise to her feet. Swiftly he grasped her wrist and pulled her down again.

'Stay here, sweetheart,' he murmured, and she had to fight to subdue her anger.

'I must check on things,' she managed to say, and after a slight hesitation he released her.

'Everything seems fine to me,' he said, and Fleur, angry and distressed, thought she detected a sardonic note in his voice.

She managed to avoid him for the next hour, smiling brightly at Steve when he claimed her to dance. She was with him again when she saw Russell, a short leather jacket draped negligently across his shoulders, taking leave of Anne. Suddenly her heart felt leaden, but she determinedly looked away, chatted eagerly to Steve, and made no attempt to go towards him.

It was much later before all the other guests departed. David offered to stay to clear some of the debris, and bleakly Fleur heard Steve saying he would help too. Anne busied herself making coffee while they collected glasses and plates, and sorting bottles.

'I'll take the empties to the bottle bank later today,' David said. 'Is the coffee ready yet?'

'Yes, let's do the rest tomorrow. Is there much food left?' Anne added as she deposited a tray near the fire.

'Are you still hungry?' Fleur asked in astonishment. 'There's enough here to feed us for several days.'

'I'm starving,' Anne confessed. 'I never manage to eat much at my own parties. Thanks, David,' she added as he reached for a plate which still had slices of pizza on it.

They sipped the coffee, tired but still keyed up, and discussed the party, but no-one made any reference to the surprising presence of Russell Delaney until half an hour later, when Anne had determinedly sent the men on their way, and came into Fleur's bedroom and plumped herself down on the bed.

Fleur was in her nightdress, carefully removing her make up.

'What brought him here?' she demanded.

'He invited himself, in a way,' Fleur explained. 'I never thought he'd come. He's spending New Year with the Kingsleys.'

Anne frowned. 'If he's made it up with Rowena what's he doing here, making such a dead set at you?' she asked angrily. 'Do you realise he didn't dance with anyone else, he barely spoke to any of the other girls, and when he wasn't with you or on his own just looking at you he was talking to the men.'

'Chad's will be alive with gossip,' Fleur said despondently.

'And you'll be here alone at Christmas,' Anne said. 'Would you like me to stay?'

'Of course not!' Fleur responded, smiling gratefully at her friend. 'It's sweet of you to suggest it, but I'll be OK.'

'It wouldn't be the sort of sacrifice you imagine,' Anne reminded her, 'since David's on duty. Steve's going to stay with his brother. But I'll ask David to keep an eye on you.'

Fleur laughed shakily and tried to make light of her fears.

'I'll be OK, truly. Now we must go to bed, there's a lot to do tomorrow.'

To her surprise she slept dreamlessly, and by Monday morning her fears seemed ridiculous. She had exaggerated everything, even Russell's attentions. She went into work with only the slightest apprehension about the expected gossip.

Most of her friends on the ward had been at the party, and beyond saying thank you and what a fabulous party it had been, they made no further remarks, even when Russell appeared to make his pre-operative tests on a new patient due for a gastrectomy.

He nodded to Fleur but seemed pre-occupied, making no attempt to speak to her. She sighed with relief, and apart from a few curious looks from others who had not been at the party, nothing extraordinary seemed to be happening.

She finished at the same time as Anne for once and they caught the same bus home.

'I saw Rowena today,' Anne said abruptly. 'She wasn't wearing her ring, and she's still in a lousy temper.'

'I don't understand,' Fleur replied. 'They must still be engaged if he's spending the holiday with her family. Perhaps the ring is too big, or something, and is being changed.'

'It's been rather a long time for that,' Anne remarked.

'Why don't you ask him, tell him you don't want anything to do with him while he's engaged to someone else.'

'I suppose I must,' Fleur said reluctantly. 'He seems more reasonable now, but it's an incredibly difficult topic to introduce. If he's after another conquest he'll be delighted to think I'm reading more into what he does than is intended.'

'You must,' Anne insisted.

'When? I can hardly approach him in the canteen and demand to know his intentions, like a Victorian father.'

'Just tell him you don't want anything more to do with him,' Anne recommended, unlocking the door into the block of flats. 'Gosh, what on earth?' she exclaimed, seeing two huge bouquets on the table where their post was left.

Fleur was reading the labels attached. 'Roses,' she said in a hollow voice. 'White for you and red for me. From Russell

Delaney. And look at this,' she added, handing Anne a note attached to her own label.

Anne read it and looked up, frowning. 'You'll be able to tell him to get lost very soon. He says he's calling for you at eight.'

SEVEN

'He-he'll make me,' Fleur said in a low voice. 'I don't know how, but he will!'

Anne stared in astonishment. 'What on earth do you mean?'

Hesitantly, Fleur explained. 'I truly didn't mean to,' she repeated. 'I was determined to come home, then I was in the Crown. I didn't mean to go near his car, but I let him take me to a restaurant, and there was nothing I could do.'

'What happened?' Anne demanded apprehensively.

'Nothing, he didn't even try to kiss me. In fact,' she confessed, 'I enjoyed myself. He's good company.'

'You've fallen for him,' Anne accused.

'No!' Fleur denied, but she knew Anne was right. Her feelings for Russell Delaney were still confused, but love had replaced the detestation she had at first felt for him.

'He's no good for you,' Anne said urgently. 'Whether he's engaged to Rowena or not, he's dangerous. Think of the stories about girls he's had fun with, but they've taken him seriously and been hurt. Fleur, try to forget him!'

'That's what I'd like to do, but I can't,' Fleur groaned.

'Are you going with him?'

'No. I don't want to, but he'll persuade me, like he did before, and this time—he might want more.'

'Then you'd better not be here when he comes. Come with us, we're going to see that new film.'

Reluctantly Fleur agreed. She hated to intrude on Anne and David, but she was terrified of not being able to resist Russell. She couldn't rely on herself to ignore the doorbell or the phone, so at half past seven she went to Leicester Square.

The film was a blur, and she wondered all the time how Russell would react when he discovered the empty flat.

'You might have had a genuine date, or come home after he called,' Anne tried to comfort her. 'It was arrogant and unreasonable of him to assume you'd be waiting for him to call.'

'I know, but it doesn't make me feel better,' Fleur said tiredly. 'He can read my thoughts before I know what I'm going to say or do. I wish I'd never set eyes on him!'

She had been avoiding Steve too, making excuses when he asked her out, but when at lunchtime he suggested a drink at the Crown that evening she accepted. She thought this would keep her safe, if she were with Steve Russell could hardly whisk her off.

They were leaving the canteen when, to her dismay, Fleur saw Russell coming towards them. He raised his eyebrows slightly, glanced from one to the other, and began to speak to Steve.

'I'm worried about that haemorrhoidectomy we did yesterday, can you come and see the chap now?' he asked, and Steve nodded, pleased to be consulted. Jealous as he was of Russell's attentions to Fleur, he still admired his skill as a surgeon.

'Right with you. See you tonight then, Fleur.'

They left together, and Fleur continued on her way. Would that be a hint to Russell? Would competition spur him on or would he totally ignore it? Somehow she thought the last was the most probable reaction. He was so supremely self-confident he would consider Fleur's preferences or Steve's interest of the least importance compared with his own wishes.

It was later that week, and she had not seen Russell again, when Fleur realised she was once more the subject of Chad's gossip. She received odd looks, and when she took some notes to Mr Havelock's office Rowena was abrupt to the point of rudeness, turning away almost before Fleur had finished giving her brief message. A couple of conversations were abruptly cut off when she appeared, and Gilly Massingham, the student she had once chastised for carelessness, and who had been antagonistic towards her ever since, eyed her with a look of unconcealed glee when they met in the corridor, and some of the first year students took to giggling and turning their backs when they saw her.

'What is it now?' she asked Anne that evening.

Anne was worried. 'I don't know,' she said slowly. 'There is something, but everyone knows we share a flat, and being extra careful not to talk in front of me. I think David's heard something, but he's being irritating, saying it's all nonsense and will blow over.'

'If it's about me, haven't I the right to know?' Fleur demanded. 'I need to know, if only to be able to deny whatever lies they're putting round about me now.'

'I'll have another go at David, though he's saying it's best to ignore gossip, because it stops sooner if you do.'

'I'll bet he wouldn't take that attitude if it was lies about him!'

'Won't Jenny tell you?'

'She's on nights, I haven't seen her this week apart from handing over and we're too rushed then to talk. I'll tackle Sue in the morning, she's sensible and will see my point of view.'

She went to the orthopaedic ward during her lunch break to find Sue, who was busy with a staff shortage and extra patients.

'I'd rather not talk here,' she answered when Fleur hesitantly explained what she wanted. 'Can we go somewhere afterwards? Not the Crown, somewhere away from the area.'

'OK. I finish at four today.'

'So will I, with luck. See you in the locker room.'

Fleur had to contain her growing curiosity and anger for the rest of the day, but eventually she was free. She changed, and sat down to wait for Sue. By half past four she was wondering if Sue had regretted her promise, but just as she had decided to wait no longer Sue appeared.

'Fleur! Thank goodness, I thought you might have gone. I'm sorry, but we had to send one of the girls off sick, and I had to wait for an agency nurse, we're so short of staff.'

She was struggling out of her uniform as she spoke, and pulling on jeans and a thick sweater. Pushing her hands through her hair to loosen it, she smiled comfortingly at Fleur and picked up an ancient duffle coat.

'Come on, I know a small discreet coffee bar.'

It was busy serving cheap meals, but they found a corner table free and Sue ordered coffee.

'Right?' Fleur had contained her impatience but now she wanted no more delay. 'What is it everyone is saying about me?'

'It's more details to the earlier story,' Sue said bluntly. 'People realised that you couldn't have been sacked from St John's, but now they've heard that a man, a patient, claimed he wanted to marry you when he was delirious.'

Fleur went cold with shock. Almost the same words as when she had told Russell about her nickname. No-one else at Chad's knew except Anne, for Steve had not been at St John's then and he would know nothing of how she had acquired her hated nickname.

'So?' She said hoarsely. 'That's not a crime on my part!'

'Then it's true?'

'Yes. But that's not enough to cause all these whispers.'

'It isn't,' Sue went on doggedly. 'They say he was old, very sick, and very rich, you tried to hold him to his offer of marriage, but his son paid you off.'

Fleur was staring at her, horror-struck. 'That's totally untrue,' she gasped. 'We laughed about it when he was better. He left hospital a couple of weeks later. He didn't have a son.'

'There's more,' Sue warned.

'Go on,' Fleur said grimly.

'You flirted with the male patients, and when you were reprimanded after one of their wives complained, a senior consultant prevented it. You can imagine what they say about his motives for intervening, suggesting he was something more to you than anyone had previously suspected.'

'It's all utterly untrue!' Fleur protested, biting her lower lip to stop it from trembling. 'No patient's wife complained. A sister did, but she was jealous, and they couldn't prove I'd been more than normally friendly with any of the patients because I hadn't! She was always looking for faults.'

'Someone's trying to damage your reputation here,' Sue commented slowly. 'This sister, jealous of a man.'

Fleur nodded. 'A doctor. She was angry when he took me out,' she said briefly, seeing no point in mentioning Steve Markham. That might involve him in the rumours.

'Then could it be someone here who's jealous?' Sue asked. 'It's been noticed

Russell Delaney is smitten,' she added. 'It could be Rowena Kingsley, no-one seems to know whether that engagement is on or off, but she's in a foul mood these days. But there are dozens of little idiots imagining themselves in love with him, who believe that if you were out of the running he would turn to them!' she concluded scornfully.

'None of the girls here know anything, and though the details are untrue, the stupid man did propose, and Sister Beasley did report me. It has to be someone who knows that.'

And Russell did, she thought bleakly. She had told him. No-one else knew. The first rumours had started when he had been angry with her, so was it a coincidence that this second false but much more damaging rumour had surfaced a few days after she had stood him up?

'Thanks for telling me, Sue,' she said quietly. 'I'm grateful, but I'd better go home now.'

'You needed to know,' Sue said as they paid the bill. 'It's being done deliberately,' she added as they went towards the bus stop, 'and must be someone with a grudge against you. If I hear anything else, or discover where these rumours start I'll tell you, don't worry.'

'Thanks,' Fleur murmured, 'I'd appreciate that.'

'I'm sorry, I wish I could do more to help,' Sue exclaimed, 'I'll say it's untrue, but you know how people would rather believe the rumours.'

Anne was indignant when Fleur explained how Russell was the only person who could have started these fresh rumours.

'Steve might have known,' she suggested tentatively, 'and of course I know the real story.'

'You'd never be so malicious as even to talk about it,' Fleur said vehemently, 'nor Steve, even if he knows much. He didn't come to St John's until afterwards.'

Anne was forced to agree, but then in an attempt to distract Fleur's thoughts from the whole nasty mess tried to interest her in Christmas shopping. 'It's almost too late to find good presents, and I haven't a clue what to give David,' she complained, but Fleur was absorbed in one matter only.

She was tempted to confront Russell but for a whole week, whenever there was a hint of an opportunity she shrank from it.

It was too embarrassing even to think of discussing it, and in any case he seemed to have given up his pursuit of her. Although he was in the ward every day he spoke only about patients.

She told herself she despised him for starting the rumours. She could think of no other way they could have appeared at Chad's, but this did not prevent Fleur's heart from contracting whenever she saw him. She grew pale and listless, dark shadows under her eyes, and a haunted look in them.

A week before Christmas there was a sudden snowstorm in the afternoon. The ground was soon covered, and when the sun appeared briefly the scene was strangely unreal as the uniform grey murkiness changed to fresh sparkling enchantment.

Fleur was on late duty, not relishing the prospect of her journey home. The temperature had dropped, and a film of ice was developing on top of the snow.

Not everyone disliked the weather. Fleur went to the children's ward late in the afternoon with a message, and those patients well enough to be up were by a window overlooking nearby rooftops. They were noisily and cheerfully making plans for slides and skating as soon as they were back home.

'We're grown up when snow stops being fun,' the senior staff nurse said to Fleur as they stood watching the excited children. 'By the way, if you're on duty on Christmas Day, try to slip in. They love visitors, poor mites, when they can't go home.'

'Will you have many here?'

'Most of these can go home, if only for a couple of days. Just the very sick, or those needing special care, have to stay. Talking of visitors, have you a moment to speak to young Sally? Her parents are divorced, and though her father comes whenever he's in London her mother can't afford to come often, she lives in Cornwall. Sally's got leukaemia, very advanced.'

'Poor little kid,' Fleur murmured, and went across to speak to a little girl lying in a bed near the door.

'I wonder if the snow will wait for me?' she asked Fleur, her eyes shining, and Fleur had great difficulty in hiding the sudden tears which threatened to choke her. She knew that the child would almost certainly never walk again, and was likely to be dead within the year.

'It will come again some day even if this lot goes quickly,' she said gently. 'It's early this year, and it's been so cold we may have lots. Try to enjoy the look of it while it's here.'

She talked for a few moments about Christmas, and how the nurses made it a special day for everyone, then said she had to go back and look after the grown up patients. She dropped a light kiss on the child's forehead and turned to leave, blinking hard to control a sudden rush of tears.

Russell was standing close behind her. Her heart gave an uncontrollable leap, and her eyes widened in sudden apprehension.

'Are you going back straight away?' he asked, looking keenly at her, and when she nodded, he turned to walk beside her.

'Why do you look so devastated whenever you see me?' he asked in a low voice as they walked along the corridor.

Fleur glanced at him. If he really did not know then he was not the sensitive, understanding man she had thought.

'Do I?' she asked, attempting to appear nonchalant.

'Yes,' he replied uncompromisingly. 'You look dreadful,' he went on in an expressionless voice. 'What's the matter?'

'I think I'm sickening for flu,' Fleur said shortly.

'I think you're evading the question, my love. Look,' he went on before she could utter the protest which hovered on the tip of her tongue at the unexpected endearment, 'it's a filthy night, I'll run you home and we can sort out a few things. I think it's time we had a straight talk. I'll see you later.'

Then he was gone, leaving Fleur's thoughts in a whirl. She was unprepared, totally incapable of deciding what to do.

When she emerged from the front entrance there was sleet falling, bitingly cold and stinging against her face. It was dark, apart from the hospital and street lighting, the wind howled round every corner, and underfoot was wet, muddy slush. When Russell appeared, taking her hand in his and guiding her towards his car, she felt only gratitude that she would have a warm, dry, comfortable and rapid journey home.

He did not speak as he negotiated the

traffic, nor suggest taking her anywhere. He drew into a rare parking space right in front of the flats, and still in silence came round and opened her door, took her hand and accompanied her to the building.

Fleur found her key, and without it being a conscious decision led him upstairs to the flat. It was in darkness and she recalled that Anne had gone to a party with David, and would be very late back. In her dazed state she did not even think of what that could mean for her, alone with Russell, but went straight into the sitting room and switched on the electric fire.

'Have you enough food, and shall I go out for a Chinese takeaway?' he asked, breaking the silence as he dropped his overcoat in the hall and followed her into the sitting room.

Fleur forced herself to concentrate. 'There's always omelette, or if you like we have some chops, and salad.'

'It all sounds delicious. Shall I cook for you?'

'I didn't know you cooked.'

'How should you? But I live alone, and I'm quite capable of providing for myself. You look exhausted. Is there any sherry?'

'In the kitchen. I'll get you some. I'm OK, thanks, quite able to cook a couple of chops.'

He followed her into the kitchen, and when she found the sherry bottle took it from her and poured two generous measures.

'Have this first,' he ordered, and Fleur began to feel some warmth stealing back into her limbs.

He perched on the kitchen table and chatted while she sprinkled herbs over the chops, grilled them and mixed a salad. He chose neutral subjects, with no amorous remarks. By the time they were sitting at the kitchen table Fleur was feeling more her normal self.

They took coffee into the sitting room, and Russell made Fleur sit opposite him, either side of the fire.

'Now, tell me what it is,' he said gently. 'Is it these silly rumours upsetting you, or is there something more?'

Fleur stared at him and all her suspicions came flooding back, wiping out the companionship of the simple dinner.

'They're untrue,' she said in a low voice.

'There's a basis of truth, magnified, vilely twisted.'

'Can't you ignore them? It's the only practical way.'

'But how do they start?' she asked angrily. 'Only a few people know the truth behind them.'

'And I do,' he said with sudden comprehension. 'No wonder you've been distant. But aren't there other possibilities?'

'Yes, of course,' she admitted slowly.

'And they are what?' he asked quietly.

'Anne knows,' Fleur said slowly, 'and Steve knows some of it, yet I can't believe either of them would try to hurt me. But only you knew everything that happened between us at St John's. And why should the rumours start every time I've made you angry?'

'What do you mean?' he asked frowning.

'They began when I refused to go out to dinner with you.'

'But I didn't expect you to accept my invitations straight away,' he said reminiscently. 'What else?'

'The second lot started after the party, when I wasn't here that night you wanted to take me out,' Fleur explained, beginning to think how silly it all sounded.

Russell did not laugh at her. 'I see. After the party I knew you might be going out with someone else, but I called here in the hope you'd be free. Surely you couldn't think I was angry about such a silly thing or would try to ruin your reputation?'

'You nearly succeeded at St John's, before you even knew me!' she pointed out tartly.

'And I'll never be forgiven,' he said with a wry grin. 'But I'm not sorry I kissed you. It was crazy, I agree, but you were irresistible. Like you are now,' he added.

He moved suddenly to kneel beside Fleur's chair, and before she could protest had taken her coffee mug away, set it down on a nearby table, and pulled her into his arms.

'My lovely, delightful Fleur,' he whispered into her hair. 'I hate to see you unhappy, my darling. It hurts, as it hurts to think that you could even suspect me of such despicable behaviour. But I suppose you don't know me well enough, and the first impressions, from your point of view, were not exactly propitious! We'll have to make sure that we get to know one another properly, as soon as possible.'

EIGHT

As Russell's lips captured hers Fleur tried to twist away, but he had moved too quickly for her, and she was a prisoner.

Knowing she was alone in the flat with him, and Anne would not be home for hours, her heart thudded in panic and she struggled to push him away. Her hands beat against his chest but he leant closer, pressing her back. The feel of his arms, strong and protective about her slender body, and the touch of his lips, warm and soft and insistent on hers, made her senses swim.

She gradually forgot everything except how utterly right it felt to be here, enfolded in Russell's arms, with his mouth teasing hers into a response.

His hair was crisp and vital, she found, as her hands slid round his neck and her fingers entwined themselves in his curls. His eyes were a deeper blue than she had thought, and she read without difficulty the message of desire in them.

When he released her for a moment and rose to his feet she felt deserted, but he stooped and lifted her from the chair, carried her across the room to the settee, and sat down with her curled up in his lap, her head cradled against his shoulder.

'My poor darling,' he murmured. 'If I'd known what misery those stupid rumours had caused you, I'd have forced you into this explanation earlier. Even if it had meant kidnapping you! That would really have given them something to gossip about!'

'I know they're not true,' she said slowly, her voice trembling, 'but who hates me enough to spread such lies?'

'Is it useless to tell you to ignore them?' he asked. 'I do, and there have been plenty of false rumours about me. It makes life much more bearable.'

Fleur blinked, and then pushed herself away from him and into a sitting position.

'Then—it's not true?' she asked, an incredulous, joyful hope beginning to grip her.

'What isn't true?' he asked, puzzled, pulling her down into his arms and slowly, with infinite care, bending to kiss the tip of her nose, her eyes, and finally again her mouth.

Fleur struggled to hold on to reality. It was amazingly difficult not to abandon herself to the bliss of his presence, the wonder of being in his arms, the delights of his embraces.

'The latest rumour about you,' she said, and then, when he looked genuinely puzzled, she overcame her sudden reluctance and spoke Rowena's name. 'That you and Rowena Kingsley are engaged.'

'That was ages ago!' he exclaimed. 'Is that still around?'

Fleur nodded. 'No-one knows, she isn't wearing her ring,' she explained shyly.

He frowned, and Fleur shivered at the grim look on his face.

'I'm not engaged to Rowena, or anyone else,' he said carefully. 'Is that another reason why you've avoided me?'

As she nodded again he suddenly grinned. 'Yes, I can see that these rumours are dangerous. It's hardly a question a girl can ask her date. Are you promised to someone else, sir? Because if you are I prefer not to have anything to do with you,' he mimicked in a falsetto voice.

'But she was wearing a ring,' Fleur pointed out defensively.

'And now she isn't. She thinks she's doing the right thing. But I'm not interested in Rowena. What of us? Can you believe that I didn't start those rumours about you?'

Slowly she nodded.

'Good. Sweetheart, there are all sorts of ways people could get hold of the story, and I suspect someone is deliberately trying to make things unpleasant. But it can't be any more than that, and no doubt all due to jealousy. A lot of girls would like to be as beautiful as you, my love.'

Soon Fleur decided that she did not in the least care about how or why the rumours had started. The only thing that mattered was being in Russell's arms, his lips on hers. They spoke little, content just to be close. At eleven o'clock Russell put her gently away from him and rose to his feet.

'Time for me to go, darling. You have to be up early. What time do you finish tomorrow?'

'I have a free afternoon.'

'I can't get away until six. I'll call for you here about seven. I'll see if I can get

127

theatre tickets, but it's close to Christmas. Are you going to the Christmas Ball?'

'No,' Fleur replied. Steve had asked her but she had refused. She didn't want them to appear closer than they actually were. No such consideration entered her head when Russell invited her.

When he had gone she began to wonder if she had dreamed it all. But a subtle fragrance remained of Russell's aftershave, there were two used dinner plates in the kitchen, and he had left a card with his private address and telephone number.

'You can always leave a message on my machine if I'm out,' he had said. 'And I can phone in and record a message, so that if I'm ever prevented from contacting you or don't turn up when you expect me, I can let you know what's happening.'

She went to bed blissfully happy, slipping the card under her pillow. She did not analyse her emotions, but suddenly the world was the marvellous, wonderful, excitingly satisfying place she had hoped to find.

At Chad's she tackled all the morning tasks with renewed energy, getting the patients settled for the day, dealing with drugs and dressings, making routine observations and preparing one new patient for theatre, and generally looking so unusually happy that Sister Reynolds commented on it.

'I'm so thankful to see you back to normal, Nurse Tremaine,' she said when they were in the office together. 'I've been afraid you were sickening for something.'

'I did feel low, probably a mild dose of flu,' Fleur said, but she coloured and could not prevent the slight smile from hovering on her lips, or disguise the brightness of her eyes.

'I rather think you have caught something,' Sister said quietly. 'I only hope he's good to you and doesn't let you down,' she added as Fleur blushed vividly.

When Fleur finished her duty she hurried straight into the West End to join the last minute Christmas shoppers. She had no ball dress remotely special enough for Russell Delaney, and she also needed to buy him a Christmas present.

The dress was easy. Fleur no sooner set eyes on it that she knew she must have it. Fortunately it was her size and just within her maximum price. Guiltily she suspected that even if it had been far more than the total amount of her savings she would have been utterly reckless and still bought it.

In a soft jade green shade, the closely fitting bodice rose out of layers of floating net. Held up by tiny shoulder straps, the skirt draperies fell in points to ankle length. She had silver sandals and evening bag, and a Victorian jade pendant which had belonged to her grandmother, which would go perfectly with it.

Anne had a dramatic black velvet cloak, and Fleur knew that she would be only too pleased to lend it to her.

She then looked for a present for Russell. This was far more difficult. If she had known him for longer she would have had some idea of his tastes, and she must not buy anything too vulgarly expensive or intimate.

She looked at and rejected wallets, leather gloves, books, and sweaters, presents she would have bought for her father. For Russell it had to be special. She was almost in despair when, passing the window of an antiquarian bookseller, she noticed some old picture maps in the back. The one which caught her eye was of the Welsh border country, with a multitude of castles drawn in, and tiny pictures of battles and sieges.

She recalled Russell's talk of his childhood, and his fantasies built around these very castles. If she had enough money it would make the perfect present. Hesitantly she asked the price, and was coldly informed by a rather superior angular woman that it was just a print. Which was fortunate, she thought in amusement as she bore her trophy homewards, carefully rolled up and protected by a cardboard cylinder, for she had only just been able to afford it. Goodness knows what originals cost.

She had spent so long shopping that it was half past six when she got home. She took a rapid shower, and was slipping a sleek black dress over her head when Anne came in.

'Hi, there,' Anne called, and a moment later she came into Fleur's room. 'Oh, I hadn't realised you were going out.'

'You weren't up this morning,' Fleur said. 'Have a good time last night?'

'So—so. It wasn't very lively. I think everyone's tired so near Christmas. I shall be glad to get home.'

'Oh, that reminds me, can I borrow your velvet cloak?'

'Sure. Have you decided to go to the ball with Steve?'

'No,' Fleur said slowly, blushing.

Anne looked sharply at her. 'Fleur, what is it?'

Fleur gulped. This was far more difficult than she had anticipated, though why it should be she could not think.

'I'm going with Russell,' she said in a small voice. 'Anne, he'll be here in a few minutes! I'll explain later.'

'I can't wait,' Anne said slowly.

'Please, if he comes before I'm ready, give him a drink,' she asked, beginning to brush her hair until it gleamed.

At that moment the doorbell pealed and Anne, with a thoughtful look at Fleur, went to answer it.

It was Russell, and when Fleur entered the sitting room she found him holding a glass of sherry and listening to Anne's eager chatter. She came out of her bemused state for long enough to smile at the way he had so instantly charmed her friend away from her inclination to be censorious, then felt her heart somersault as he rose swiftly to his feet, put down his glass, and crossed the room to meet her, his hands descending on her shoulders and his lips lightly caressing hers.

'You're lovely, and punctual, my darling,' he laughed.

Fleur smiled, and then her smile deepened impishly at Anne's startled look. She was used to men like Steve and David who were far more restrained, and took time to reach the stage of kissing in public. No doubt Anne was thinking of Russell's reputation, wondering if it was this technique which had won it for him.

For a moment Fleur's smile wavered as she thought of those many other girls, then she shrugged. How could anyone feel so incomplete without him and so naturally right together, if her love was not returned? He could not behave as he did unless he loved her.

'We must go, I've tickets for the National. I hope you have a good holiday,' he said to Anne, who murmured some inaudible response as they went.

Fleur could not remember afterwards what the play was, only that she sat in a glow of contentment, seeing and hearing what happened on stage, but not following a single thread of the plot. During the interval they listened to carol singers in the foyer, and Russell introduced Fleur to some friends who looked at her with interest. They were not connected with Chad's or medicine, but she did not catch their names or remember the conversation.

Afterwards Russell drove to a small restaurant in Covent Garden and at midnight they arrived back at the flat.

'I won't come in, it's too late,' he whispered as he pulled her to him and kissed her lingeringly. 'I'm on duty tomorrow night, but I'll pick you up at eight the next day and we'll have dinner before the ball. Sleep well, my love.'

Fleur let herself in, dazed with happiness, and found Anne in a shabby old dressing gown, asleep in a chair by the fire.

She woke and stretched when Fleur came in, and looked quickly past her into the hall.

'It's OK, I'm alone,' Fleur reassured her. 'Were you playing watchdog?'

'Do I need to?' Anne demanded. 'Fleur, for pity's sake, I'm eaten up with curiosity! Tell me all!'

'He's not engaged to Rowena!' Fleur said happily. 'Anne, don't you think he's fabulous?'

About to utter words of warning, Anne saw the glow of joy in Fleur's face, and bit them back. She feared that Russell would treat Fleur as one more conquest, and drop her flat when he had tired of her. That would be the time to offer comfort. Let her enjoy at least the illusion of love in the meantime.

'Tell me,' she invited again. 'Do you want some chocolate? Come into the kitchen while I make some.'

Fleur told her briefly about the previous day, and Anne hid her disquiet. She was leaving for her home in the morning, and worried that Fleur would be alone in the flat. Then she told herself not to be a fool. Fleur could fend for herself, and was old enough to know what she was doing if she allowed this affair to proceed as fast as it looked like doing. Besides, Fleur was so deeply enchanted that she would not heed any warnings.

It was the fear that Fleur could be on her own when the inevitable crash came that concerned Anne, then she shrugged. Even Russell Delaney was unlikely to tire of her in a week, and then Fleur was going home for the New Year. Afterwards Anne would also be back, to help pick up the pieces when the inevitable break happened.

'We must go to bed,' she said suddenly.

'Wake me up before you go out, I've so much to do before I catch the train.'

They parted early the next morning with mutual good wishes and exchange of wrapped parcels.

'Not to be opened before Christmas Day, remember,' Fleur said with a laugh.

Anne grinned. 'I learned that lesson when I was ten. I found all the presents one day when my parents were out and my sister glued to the television. They hadn't been wrapped and I peeped into all of them, and was so disappointed when there were no surprises on Christmas Day. Give my love to your parents. Heavens, is that the time? You'll be late. Take care.'

Fleur drifted through the day on a cloud. She kept her eyes demurely lowered when Russell came round the ward, but he treated her exactly as he did all the nurses, not betraying by the flicker of an eyelid that they had a life outside the hospital. For a moment she was taken aback, and then smiled to herself. He was obviously taking great care not to start any more rumours. Yet by the following night, when they had been at the hospital ball together, the grapevine would once more be busy.

By the greatest good fortune she had the next two days off, to prepare in a leisurely manner for the ball and recover from it the day after. She had her hair shaped, then soaked in a steaming bath to which she added a generous amount of lemon-scented bath gel, before doing her nails. She was ready, tense with nerves, a full quarter of an hour before Russell was due.

He was exactly on time and Fleur quivered with emotion when she opened the door. He was so superb, so handsome and elegant in evening dress, and he loved her. She was certain of that, and the embrace he held her in for long minutes would have told her that he was as moved as she was by their meeting.

'I could stay here with you in my arms all night,' he said huskily. 'But I want to display my utterly beautiful, gorgeous Fleur to everyone. Come, we'll have to go.'

They dined at a small French restaurant, unimpressive from the outside, but providing perfectly cooked and well served food in an elegant setting. Russell was obviously well known, and Fleur suffered a spark of jealousy. How many other girls had he brought here? Then she told herself not to be foolish. He was over thirty and attractive. There must have been many girls in his life before her. She would be thoroughly miserable if she spent all her time thinking about them.

When they reached the hotel where the ball was being held the dancing was in full swing. Fleur went to leave her cloak, then they went up to the ballroom and he immediately swung her onto the floor, holding her closely and leading her expertly through the throng of other dancers.

Fleur loved dancing, and gave herself up to the sheer bliss of a skilful partner. Too often her escorts considered that if they held her closely without treading on her toes they had performed creditably.

She was so absorbed that it was not until the music stopped and Russell reluctantly removed his arm from around her waist that she realised how many people were looking at her. They wore a variety of expressions, surprise, envy, amusement, and in some faces rather unpleasant speculation.

Russell was sublimely indifferent. He was flatteringly attentive, and although he ensured that they mingled with others, and introduced Fleur to many of the senior staff, who until now had been only names, or occasionally faces to her, his tender and protective attitude demonstrated to everyone that he was most content when he was dancing with or talking alone to Fleur.

Just one incident marred an otherwise perfect evening. At midnight, when some of the older consultants were beginning to drift away, Rowena Kingsley appeared with a strange man.

She was dressed in black, a tight, daringly low dress slit to the thigh. She was not incapably drunk, but it was obvious both she and her companion had been drinking steadily. Rowena stared about her as she entered the ballroom, saw Russell and Fleur and said something to her companion.

Then she began to move purposefully in their direction. The man caught her arm and seemed to be arguing with her, then as she tried to pull away jerked her roughly round and almost dragged her across the room.

Fleur had seen all of this, as she had been facing the door. Russell became aware of it when the obvious interest of Fleur and others caused him to swing round in time to see the struggle.

Fleur heard him mutter to himself as he half rose to his feet, his face grim, and then he paused.

'She'll go to the devil in her own way, I suppose,' he said with a shrug, sitting down again. 'Sorry, darling.'

'Who is he?' Fleur asked, suddenly cold with apprehension. 'Is he a doctor? I haven't seen him before,' she went on, anxious not to drop into a betraying silence.

'He left a few months back, went to a private clinic. Although he doesn't look capable of it now, he's a top plastic surgeon. But he's an unscrupulous hound with women,' he added bitterly. 'I feel I ought to drag her away by force, but I'd probably do harm by interfering. Let's dance again.'

It was a slow, dreamy waltz, and he held her close, his cheek resting on her head. Fleur felt too petrified to think clearly, for his reaction to Rowena had undermined all her own delight in what she had assumed were Russell's feelings for her. Now she was much less certain of him or his motives for paying her such lavish attention.

With a determined effort she pushed the nagging worries from her conscious thoughts. Russell's attentions finally drove away all memory of Rowena until, at an early hour in the morning, he left her at the door of the flat.

'I daren't come in,' were his parting words as he held her closely and kissed her with a greater degree of passion than he had displayed before. 'If I did you'd never get me out again. How could I have existed without you? It wasn't a complete life, that I know. Goodnight, my beloved.'

NINE

Fleur slept dreamlessly for a few hours, then a noise in the street woke her and she lay in bed wondering why she felt a sense of impending gloom when she ought to be in seventh heaven.

She shivered, and tried to blot out the unformed but overwhelming fear in her mind. It was impossible to sink back into oblivion, despite her short sleep, so she got up, pulled on some old clothes, made coffee and toast, and sat huddled in front of the sitting room fire.

She felt bitterly cold, despite a thick sweater on top of a long sleeved Viyella shirt. Outside the wintry sun was shining, but the bare branches of the lime trees hung motionless. The cold was within her, and she finally faced the question why.

Carefully, she went over all her conversations with Russell, trying to isolate what frightened her. She realised with a sick feeling of despair that although he had said plainly that he was not engaged to Rowena, he had not said that he had never been engaged to her. And his instinctive reaction the previous night showed clearly she still meant a great deal to him. Did he want her back, or was he angry to see her with a man he disliked? Was he jealous?

With that thought came the devastating suspicion that he might be using her to make Rowena jealous. Fleur was not vain, and Rowena was exceptionally beautiful.

'No-one could really prefer me to her,' she whispered.

And his endearments? They were extravagant. Was it his habit with women, or was such caressing language a deliberate ploy? He had never actually committed himself to an outright declaration of love although he called her his love and his darling and similar intimate and tender names.

He desired her, but men often desired women without being in love with them. There had been plenty of warnings in his reputation for sudden romances, swiftly undertaken and as abruptly ended. Why should she consider herself different from the many other girls who had come into his orbit?

Rowena was different. She now felt sure that he had been engaged to her. Suddenly she realised that he had never denied starting the rumours about her, or satisfactorily explained how else they could have started.

She forced herself to review the few occasions when she had seen them together after the engagement was broken, for now she was convinced that was the truth. Rowena had always looked furious, and Russell grim. Quite natural in the circumstances. Perhaps from the reports of Rowena's bad temper she was regretting it and only pride stopped her from trying to make up the quarrel, while he was taking his own unscrupulous measures to resolve it.

Blinking back tears, Fleur angrily told herself she was a fool. Sitting there glooming would not be of the slightest use. When he came this evening, as he promised, she would tell him to go away again, because she did not care to be used to goad Rowena into making up whatever quarrel they had had.

She needed to direct her fury into something energetic, so exhausting that she would sleep from sheer weariness that night. It was a pleasant day, and she could take a long walk, but the prospect was uninviting. It would not occupy her thoughts.

In the end she decided to decorate her own bedroom. The dingy wallpaper had always depressed her.

She moved her things into Anne's room and pushed the bed and the wardrobe into the centre of the room. Covering them with a sheet she set to, attacking the old wallpaper vigorously, and found it an excellent way of utilising her fury against Russell.

She stopped briefly for a sandwich and coffee, then realised that the shops would soon be shut for Christmas and she must buy what she needed now. She couldn't leave the flat disorganised for Anne to come back to.

She went out to the nearest shopping parade and found some very pretty wallpaper with tiny blue flowers on a white background. Fleur bought several rolls as well as paint and brushes and wallpaper paste.

Laden with her parcels, she belatedly thought about food for the holiday and hastily collected stores from the super-market.

Back in the flat she glanced at the cooker clock. Three o'clock. Good, she could do at least three more hours before she need tidy herself up to deal with Russell. She had no intention of dressing up for him, of course, she told herself angrily, but she would feel more equipped to tell him that she did not wish to see him again if she had bathed and changed.

It would be a lie. She did want to see him again, but to continue as they were would only hurt more in the end, which must be an inevitable parting.

She set herself grimly to finish scraping. Previous tenants had put new paper on top of old, with four different layers in some places. But soon only the last wall remained. She would do that on the following evening, or even finish it tonight after she had sent Russell away.

She suddenly realised that she had no idea of the time. It had grown dark ages ago. She sped into the kitchen and gasped with dismay. The cooker clock still said three o'clock.

Fleur ran into Anne's bedroom, forgot for a few moments where she had put her watch, and then began to scrabble for it amongst the mound of small items she had dropped on top of the dressing table, intending to sort them out later. When she retrieved her watch she groaned. It was twenty-five past seven and Russell had said he would be there at seven. He was late.

Perhaps he wasn't coming. Perhaps taking her to the ball had brought him and Rowena together, wondering how they could have been so crazy as to split up.

Instead of being relieved at escaping a quarrel, Fleur was overwhelmed with anguish. He was not coming!

To still the sudden trembling in her legs she went into the kitchen, poured herself, rather unsteadily, a large gin, splashed a token teaspoonful of orange juice into it, and gulped nervously. She sat at the kitchen table, a bleak look on her face, and suddenly felt tears trickling down her cheeks.

'Damn him! Damn him! Damn him!' she whispered, angrily brushing them away with the back of her hand, and drank the rest of the gin in one swallow.

She was still trying to recover her breath when the doorbell rang. Her heart leapt. He was here, he had not deserted her! Then she realised that she would have to face him after all and suddenly felt cold. The bell pealed again and slowly, her pulses throbbing, she went to open the door.

Russell stood there, unexpectedly dressed in jeans and a heavy fisherman's sweater. He carried a bottle of wine wrapped in festive green and red paper and a small white carrier bag.

His eyebrows shot up and his lips curved in amusement as he surveyed Fleur in her old jeans, hair and shirt spattered with drips of dirty water and with shreds of clinging old wallpaper.

He went past her, ignoring the instinctive

147

movement of her hand as she tried to bar the way, and deposited his parcels on the kitchen table. Then he turned and surveyed her closely before walking back and taking both her hands in his.

'What is it, sweet?' he asked gently, and Fleur stared up into his eyes, noting the concern in them, and wondered whether she was utterly crazy to harbour such dreadful suspicions about him. 'I'm sorry I'm late, there was an emergency operation, a road accident and peritonitis from a wound. Had you given me up?' he asked, surveying her old clothes.

'Of course not!' she retorted, angry that he should think a mere half hour's lateness could cause such distress. 'I—you—it's nothing,' she stammered.

She tried to pull her hands away, but his slim fingers gripped her effortlessly and she could not escape. Then he relaxed his hold and moved one hand up to her face.

'What is it?' he asked gently, his fingers tracing the path her tears had worn in her dusty face.

She shook her head wordlessly.

'I thought you might be too tired to

go out again, especially as Sir John Summers asked me to bring you to his party tomorrow night, so I bought a Chinese takeaway and some wine,' he said calmly. 'Sit down, it's all ready,' he went on, swiftly putting several small plastic containers from the carrier bag on the table. He picked up the glass she had used for the gin, paused for a moment, then moved it to the drainer without comment, just casting her a worried look.

Bemused, Fleur sat and watched as he found plates, cutlery and glasses, then removed the lids of the containers, shared out the contents and poured wine into the glasses.

'Here, eat while it's hot,' he ordered, pushing one of the plates in front of her and putting a fork into her hand.

Mechanically she obeyed, and suddenly found herself excessively hungry. She had been working hard all day and eaten almost nothing, and the tasty sweet and sour chicken, stir fried vegetables, and fluffy saffron-tinted rice were delicious. She drank some wine, then realised that it was champagne. Odd, she mused, she had never before seen anyone remove a champagne cork without popping it. And why had he brought champagne, she suddenly wondered.

She glanced up at him, but he was not looking at her. However, he began to tell her the details of an unusual case he had operated on that morning, and one part of her mind was caught. She had never seen the removal of a bile duct tumour, and would be concerned with the post-operative care of the patient on the following day.

'How long is she likely to be in bed?' she asked, and did not notice the look of satisfaction in his eyes that she had broken her silence.

He talked easily, and Fleur did not notice how often he refilled her glass. When he cleared away the plates and dumped the containers in the waste bin, she rose to find cheese and biscuits, apologising that it was all she had. Then she made coffee and he carried the tray into the sitting room. They were installed in armchairs opposite one another, sipping the fragrant brew, before he spoke.

'Can you tell me now what's the matter?' he asked gently.

Fleur glanced across at him, a haunted look in her eyes. Could he be a deceitful, conniving philanderer, totally careless of any hurt he might cause his victims, when he looked at her like this? And when he had given her time to recover her poise, making her eat, chatting about neutral things, without demanding a word of explanation until now.

She could not pour out all her hateful suspicions. In his absence she had persuaded herself to believe the worse of him but now, while he was here, regarding her so anxiously, and with the same loving care of her that she had grown to associate with him, she could not believe them. Utterly confused, she shook her head. She could not tell him lies, or find some excuse for her attitude.

'Please, I'm being stupid,' she said in a low voice. 'Forgive me, but I'd rather not talk about it. I really am better now,' she added to forestall further questions.

To her astonishment and deep relief, he accepted this.

'As you wish. What have you been doing, decorating?'

Fleur for the first time recalled what a sight she must look, and her hand strayed to her hair. It was too tangled to put it right with a few pats, and she smiled ruefully.

'I always mean to wear a shower cap,' she said resignedly, 'and always forget. I decided to repaper my bedroom while Anne was away,' she explained, and then apologetically: 'I hadn't forgotten you were coming, but the clock had stopped and I'd lost track of time.'

'Then it's fortunate I hadn't tickets for some early show,' he teased lightly. 'How is it going? Are you finding lots of other jobs which need doing as well?'

'Something like that. Mainly the number of layers of old wallpaper, but I've done three walls. I can soon do the rest tomorrow night, and start papering over Christmas. Luckily the paintwork's reasonable, just needs a good scrub and one coat.'

'It sounds a big job,' he responded easily, ignoring the hint that she was not intending to go with him to the party he had mentioned, even though Sir John Summers was one of the most important consultants at Chad's, and it was a social triumph to have been invited to his home.

'I'm in old clothes, so I'll help you finish scraping.'

'I've only one scraper,' Fleur said, astonished. Somehow Russell had seemed to her the embodiment of the sophisticated surgeon, and she had never imagined him a house repair expert.

'I did my own flat,' he said, 'I'll do the scraping while you wash the paintwork. Then it'll be dry by tomorrow.'

Because it would occupy the rest of the evening and save her from having to offer any explanation for her odd behaviour, Fleur accepted. She could not talk about it yet, she told herself in panic. His presence had thrown all her painful conclusions into disarray. Although she was too terrified to hope she'd been wrong, she dared not try to resolve her doubts by talking to Russell about them.

Not yet, she said silently as she collected rags and a bucket of hot soapy water, while he set about the final stubbornly clinging wallpaper. She needed more time to consider everything. And perhaps, a small voice within her whispered, he might give some clearer indication of what he really feels.

He had taken off the heavy sweater and

was working in his jeans and a thin short sleeved T-shirt. She stood for a moment in the doorway, watching the rippling muscles of his arms and back. She recalled her first sight of that back, naked and tanned, and ached with the need to run to him and be enfolded in those strong arms, to be told that her imaginings were all a ghastly nightmare and Rowena meant nothing to him.

He must have sensed her regard for her glanced over his shoulder and smiled.

'Have you heard of Ted Roberts' latest exploit?' he asked.

Ted Roberts was a houseman with a talent for devising hilarious party games for the regular social club discos. Fleur had heard of them, but not yet experienced any.

'What was that?' she asked, pulling forward a chair to stand on and begin on the paintwork round the window.

'He knew Jonty Scott was thoroughly drunk last night, but the fellow's got an amazingly hard head. Although he wouldn't operate after such a bender he does see patients. Ted dressed himself up as a woman, and got the make-up expert from the drama society to paint him so that he looked a frightful old hag. He went to Jonty's clinic this morning and persuaded the receptionist to add him to the end of the list of patients. Then he went in and pretended to be a beauty queen whose face Jonty had ruined during an operation. For a few moments Jonty actually believed him and Ted says you could see the whites of his eyes, and would have been able to if they hadn't been bloodshot.'

Fleur was frowning, uncomprehendingly. 'I'm sorry, I don't understand,' she said slowly. Russell exclaimed apologetically.

'Idiotic of me. I forgot you wouldn't remember him. Jonty is, despite his habits, an exceedingly brilliant plastic surgeon with a flourishing private practice in Harley Street.'

Fleur turned away hastily, and when she saw her distraught expression reflected in the dark glass of the uncurtained window she took a deep breath and glanced at Russell. But he had turned back to scraping, and she wondered whether it was coincidence that he should mention a plastic surgeon. That had been the speciality of Rowena's escort, and he had also recently left Chad's to set up in private practice, as well as being very much under the influence at the ball. There could not have been two drunken, brilliant plastic surgeons around, surely.

She tried to laugh, and as Russell told her more about the crazy doings of the mad Ted Roberts, found it easier. By the time they had finished work and the bedroom was ready for painting, she was almost her old self, her suspicions of Russell buried once more deep in some hidden recess of her mind.

They had coffee but he made no attempt to kiss her until, with a sigh, he rose to depart.

'I hate to leave you,' he whispered as she lifted her face to his, then he almost crushed her ribs as he pulled her into a fierce embrace, and kissed her until her pulses were rioting about her body and she was beginning to think that she would never again be able to breathe.

'My darling beloved Fleur,' he said, his voice shaking with emotion, as at last he lifted his lips from hers. 'I can't ever bear to let you go. I can hardly wait until tomorrow. I love you so very much.'

TEN

The memory of those last few words, and the hard work, ensured Fleur a peaceful night. By morning she was a sure of Russell's love as she had previously been convinced of his perfidy.

Her heart and steps were light as she worked, joking with the patients. She helped three going home for Christmas to pack their belongings, spent time encouraging the others who would spend Christmas in hospital, and directed a couple of off-duty students who had volunteered to come in and decorate the ward's Christmas tree, gift of the local Chamber of Commerce.

Half way through the morning Sister Reynolds called her into the office.

'Staff, we need Mrs Archibald's notes, she's coming in for two nights for a barium meal. She'll be here this afternoon, but Mr Havelock still has her record file after the EEG he did. Please will you go to his office and insist on having them. He may be a brilliant surgeon but his organisation is far from helpful to the rest of us,' she added tartly. 'I'm sorry to ask you, normally I'd send one of the first years, but they wouldn't have the nerve to be firm with the great man!'

Fleur grinned, and nodded. 'Yes, when I first started I was terrified to speak to anyone in a white coat, until I discovered some of them were as raw in medical school as I was a nurse. I don't mind going in the least.'

She was halfway down the corridor where the consultant surgeons and their secretaries had offices before it dawned on her that Rowena Kingsley was Mr Havelock's secretary.

She hesitated, frowning, then shrugged. Russell said he loved her, and was not going to marry Rowena, so why should she be reluctant to face the other girl? Rowena might resent her, and after the ball she would know that Russell had a new love, but he couldn't love two girls at once. Or could he?

Deciding she must be sensible and stop worrying Fleur took a deep breath and went on.

The door of the outer office where

Rowena had her desk was open. There was no-one inside but the murmur of a man's voice came from the inner room. Rowena's desk chair was pushed back, a filing cabinet drawer was open with a folder lying on top of it, and it looked as though she had been called suddenly from the room. Probably Mr Havelock was dictating.

Fleur crossed to the inner door and was about to knock when Rowena's voice, high pitched and hysterical, came clearly to her.

'Darling, I'm sorry! I'm so sorry, it was all my fault, I've been a fool! Please forgive me! I don't want to lose you, truly I don't. Can't we try again?'

Fleur retreated hastily. She could not interrupt such a scene. Belatedly as though suffering from delayed shock, she began to wonder who was with Rowena. It couldn't be Mr Havelock. A dreadful suspicion began forming in her mind, and without conscious thought she backed across the office as far as she could until brought up short by the edge of the filing cabinet.

She stared across the room, hands clenched and knuckles white. At that moment the inner door opened. Petrified,

Fleur knew that her suspicions were correct, her whole world was about to crash around her. Russell emerged from the inner office, smiling contentedly, then turned slightly in the doorway and spoke to Rowena behind him.

'Phone me in the morning, we can decide what to do about my coming to your parents. Thank heavens it's all come right.'

He turned again, and Fleur instinctively shrank back, edging round the side of the open filing cabinet, but he strode across the room without noticing her and went out. She took a few involuntary steps after him, then stopped. What could she do? She could hardly run along the corridors of Chad's demanding an explanation. There was only one explanation. He had made up his quarrel with Rowena.

Suddenly a feeling of rage swept over Fleur. The despicable, hateful man! She loathed him, and never wanted to see him again! Then she shook her head. No, that was untrue. However badly he had treated her, using her to win back Rowena, she loved him and always would.

She was standing there, a bleak look on her face, utterly forlorn, when footsteps behind her brought her back to a consciousness of where she was. She turned slowly. Rowena, a tremulous smile on her lips, her face radiant, looking even more lovely, was coming out of the inner office.

'Hello, I didn't know anyone was here. Can I do anything?' she asked cheerfully, smiling at Fleur.

Summoning up all her courage, Fleur faced this girl who had captured the man she herself had come to love, and somehow conveyed the message from Sister Reynolds.

'Oh, yes, they're in here. Sorry about that, I've been rather preoccupied the last few days,' Rowena said with another smile, going towards the filing cabinet. 'Here they are,' she added, handing a folder across to Fleur. 'Hurry on tomorrow, then I can relax for a few days. Are you working at Christmas?'

Fleur nodded, unable to speak. How could Rowena behave so insensitively. She did not appear to be gloating over a rival, and Fleur suddenly wondered if she knew that Russell had been seeing her. She had been partly drunk at the ball, or might simply not have recognised Fleur in uniform. Yet surely, even though she only came into Chad's occasionally, the hospital grapevine would have made her aware of the fact that Russell had a new girl? Or had had one, Fleur corrected her chaotic thoughts, bringing her attention back to Rowena.

'Poor you! That's one advantage of being a secretary. I'm off home this evening, just as soon as I've cleared up here. Have a really Merry Christmas.'

'Thanks, you too, I must get back,' Fleur managed.

To her relief when she got back to the ward it was time for lunch and she could escape for a while. Unable to face her friends or food, she went to the park just a short walk away. It was the only place she could think of where she could be alone. To lick her wounds, she thought dully.

It was bright and sunny, but bitterly cold, the frost still glittering on car windscreens and those areas of ground not yet touched by the sun. The lake, where small paddle boats could be hired in summer, was frozen in all but a small corner, and dozens of water birds were crowded into those few square yards, or pecking despondently at the frozen ground on the bank.

A man with a bag of crumbs was scattering them slowly around him. No sooner had the crumbs reached the ground than the ducks waddled towards them, often deprived at the very last moment when more spritely sparrows darted in to snatch up the prize.

Then the man held out his arm stiffly, a handful of crumbs tempting the birds. Fleur, who had been watching him without thought, was startled to see first one, then half a dozen sparrows fly to perch on his outstretched arm, pecking at the crumbs he held, squabbling noisily as, in their attempts to reach the food they dislodged one another.

Eventually all the food was gone and the birds departed in search of more. Fleur turned away too, it was time she went back, though how she would contrive to get through the remainder of the day she had no idea. Somehow she managed, inventing a blinding headache when Jenny commented worriedly on her pallor.

'Poor Fleur, I do hope it will soon be better. But at least you'll be less busy over Christmas, with theatres closed apart from emergencies. I'm so excited to be going home, it's my first Christmas off for three years.'

'I'll have New Year instead,' Fleur replied, 'then I can have a good rest.'

'Yes. Oh, I almost forgot. Would you be a dear and water my pot plants? They'll only need doing once, I'll give them a good soak tonight before I go.'

'Of course. Will the porter let me in?'

'I've borrowed a spare key. Thanks, I'd hate to lose them and the central heating dries them out.'

By the end of the afternoon Fleur had a genuine headache, and felt so ill that she was tempted, when an empty taxi cruised past the bus stop, to treat herself to a comfortable ride home.

Once there her instinct was to crawl into bed and try to blot out her misery, but she knew that if she did, and managed by some miracle to sleep for a while she would only wake during the night and leave herself prey to hours of sleepless agony.

She must tire herself out again, so wearily she swallowed some aspirin, soaked for a while in a hot bath to try to relax, then forced herself to grill some bacon and eggs and eat. Afterwards she changed into her old clothes and tackled the painting in her bedroom.

Russell had promised to call at eight, to take her to the party, but of course he would not now. When the phone rang at half past seven she wondered if it would be him, with either the truth or some excuse. Reluctant to discover it, panic stricken at the mere thought of talking to him, she let the phone ring. She counted twenty rings before the caller gave up, then the phone went again immediately, and this time rang for even longer.

Fleur stared at it anxiously, as if expecting it to jump up and attack her, but when it eventually fell silent again, she hastily took the receiver off the hook. She knew that if she had the bell going constantly she would sooner or later be compelled to answer it, whether she wished to or not.

At ten past eight the door bell rang. Fleur froze. She really had not expected Russell to turn up after having made it up with Rowena, but it was unlikely to be anyone else. She was just distractedly wondering whether she could ignore it, and blaming herself for not having had the wit to turn off such lights as were visible from the street, when the bell rang again.

Fleur took a deep breath. She would have to face him sometime, perhaps it would be better to do it in the privacy of the flat. She could not be sure of how she would react if she had to meet him for the first time in the corridors or canteen at Chad's. Slowly, paint brush in hand, she went to open the door.

Russell stood there, smiling unconcernedly at her, and to her dismay she saw behind him a couple she had been introduced to at the ball, Peggy and Timothy Crofton. Peggy wore a long blue dress, while the men had conventional evening dress. The people throwing the party were not the sort who would appreciate guests wearing jeans or track suits, Russell had warned Fleur, when she questioned him about the affair.

'Forgotten the time again darling?' he queried lightly, 'or had you given me up and decided to get on with some work? I'm sorry I'm late, but I couldn't get through to you on the phone, there was some faulty connection.'

Fleur looked down at her paint bespattered jeans and the old shirt of her father's which she had appropriated a long time ago and now used for dirty jobs, then back at him, confused, biting back the angry words she wanted to hurl at him. It was hardly possible to start a row with the Croftons there. She turned a puzzled look in their direction.

'Forgive us, Fleur, for bursting in on you,' Peggy said, seeing her bewilderment. 'Our car's out of action, and Russell offered us a lift. We'd have waited outside, but the most ridiculous thing happened. My shoulder strap broke. Could I possible come in and borrow a needle and cotton to mend it?'

'Of course,' Fleur said, stepping back and indicating the sitting room. 'Sorry it's a mess, I'm decorating.'

Peggy smiled at her. 'You're an angel, I didn't want to have to go all the way home again, and drag Russell there since he refused to let us take a taxi.'

Fleur crossed to where a workbox sat on a shelf.

'I think there's some blue cotton in here. Would you like to use the bedroom?'

'I can manage, thanks, it's right at the front, I don't need to take my dress off.'

'And you'll have time to get changed, forgetful one,' Russell said, his tone amused and his glance warm. 'May I offer Peggy and Timothy a drink while we wait?'

Fleur stared back at him, then realised that she was appearing rather gauche. Flushing slightly, she turned to Peggy who was busy threading a needle.

'I'm sorry. Would you like sherry? It's about all I have.'

'I'll do it,' Russell said firmly. 'Get changed, love.'

Fleur retreated to the bathroom, more to give herself time to think than because she intended obeying his commands. Absentmindedly she washed her hands and face, noting that for once, perhaps because she had been painting for a comparatively short time, they were not liberally daubed with paint. But her thoughts were all on Russell. How could he behave like this? Of course, he had not seen her in Rowena's office, so could have no idea that she had heard the other girl's words and knew all about the change in their relationship.

She went into the bedroom and almost without thinking began to take off her old clothes. Then a quiver of hope struck her. Was there any way in which she could have misinterpreted Rowena's words? She thought dazedly back over them and shook her head. No, Rowena had been apologising, begging for another chance, and from the joyous look on her face as she left the office she had been forgiven. And Russell had been there so it must have been their quarrel that was being referred to. Also he'd mentioned visiting her parents. There was no other explanation.

Why did he treat her as though nothing had happened? Did he, callously and totally without any consideration for her, intend to enjoy himself with her while Rowena was at home for Christmas? Or had he been caught by the circumstances of people knowing he was taking her to the party, so that he would not be able to tell her the truth until he could speak to her alone?

She pulled a lacy white top and a long black skirt out of the wardrobe and had actually put them on before she realised what she had done. She looked in the mirror and sat down to brush her hair, then, at last, began to wonder what she had best do. Ought she to send Russell on his way, make some excuse, or—and suddenly she knew what she was going to do.

If he could pretend so could she. The

temptation to spend one more evening in his company, to dance once more with his arms about her, to kiss him again even if she knew it was a traitor's kiss, was too great. It would be bitter sweet, but perhaps, for seconds at a time, she could forget and dream once more that when he had said he loved her he had been speaking the truth.

Fleur hastened to get ready. She never wore a great deal of make up, and tonight used only a light foundation and a minimum of eye shadow and lip gloss, so that she was back in the sitting room just as Peggy was breaking off the cotton.

'Darling Fleur, thank you so much,' Peggy exclaimed gaily. 'So embarrassing to lose my dress in the middle of the party, I'm thankful the strap gave way before we got here.'

'Have some sherry?' Russell asked, but Fleur shook her head, and they trooped down to the car, squeezed themselves in, and within a short time were entering a large, rather imposing house which overlooked the River Thames at Richmond.

'It's a pity it's not summer,' Russell said after he and Fleur had greeted their host and hostess, Sir John and Lady Summers, and been given glasses of wine by a uniformed waitress. 'There's a beautiful garden leading right down to the river, and I've been to some memorable parties here. Perhaps next summer you'll see what I mean.'

Fleur strove to keep the polite smile fixed on her face. How could he be so cruel as to imply that they would be together in the summer, when he must be intending to break with her this very evening? Then she wondered anew at his deceitfulness, and reminded herself that even if he did want to keep her in ignorance of what had happened for longer, he would be forced to break with her as soon as Rowena was back in London.

The party was crowded, Russell seemed to know everyone there. Fleur recognised many faces from Chad's, though mostly older than her friends and higher up the career ladder. Russell seemed to be in great demand, and they had no time for private conversation until some of the younger people began dancing in the largest of the interconnecting rooms.

'Come, I've been feeling deprived without you in my arms for almost twenty four hours,' Russell whispered to Fleur and, his arm about Fleur's waist, led her through to the dancing.

This was almost more than she could bear. It was slow, sensuous music, and he held her close. She felt his lips against her forehead, and wanted to break away from him and scream that he was a monster. But she did not, and it was not the surroundings that deterred her. Agonising though it was to think that this might be the last time she would experience his embrace, she knew she could not bear to lose a minute of it.

When the music ended Russell led Fleur through to another room where a buffet supper was laid out, and despite her protests loaded two plates with smoked salmon and salad. He found a quiet corner in the hall and they sat side by side on a long seat. Fleur struggled with the food while he chatted about the people there, telling her who worked at Chad's.

He seemed unaware of her silence, apart from once when he asked whether she was tired.

'No, not really, although I suppose it has all been rather a busy time,' she replied rather incoherently, and he smiled sympathetically.

'I'll get some more to drink then. Wait here, my sweet.'

It was fortunate that he left her then, to shrink back into the corner and hastily blink away the tears at his endearment. When he brought refilled glasses she quickly bent over hers, sipping slowly, until he suggested that they danced again.

'I begin to regret having offered the Croftons a lift,' he murmured softly to her. 'It was difficult not to, as they live in the same block, and he was tinkering with his car when I got home. If only we could steal away now. I want to kiss you until you're breathless, you're so temptingly beautiful.'

Fleur wanted to scream at him to stop it, but her voice seemed to have deserted her, and at that moment Sir John Summers, with quiet apologies to the people he disturbed, came into the middle of the dancers and laid his hand on Russell's arm.

'Just a moment, my boy, if you please.'

Russell looked quickly at him, then turned and followed him off the floor, his arm about Fleur's waist so that she had to go too. They were led into a tiny room which looked as though it was an office. Sir John turned to Russell

173

and without preamble spoke, quietly and sympathetically.

'I've just had a phone call from Chad's. They asked me to tell you that Miss Kingsley has been admitted and there will have to be an operation immediately.'

Fleur felt Russell's arm tighten round her like a band of steel, and he caught his breath sharply. But his voice was even when he spoke.

'What is it?' he asked quietly.

'A car crash. She apparently called in to collect something, an hour ago, and soon after she left her car skidded and crashed with a lorry. The roads are very icy.'

'Did they say what was wrong?'

'They don't know yet, but there are abdominal injuries, and they are afraid of a fractured skull.'

'Who's there?'

The other understood him immediately.

'Don't worry, my boy. Mr Havelock and Mr Fergusson. She couldn't have two better surgeons to care for her. Do you know her father's schedule? Can he be reached?'

'He'll be on his way home. He planned to get back on the twenty-third, the day after tomorrow. Shall I ring her mother?'

'I think it would be better if you went to Chad's first and saw her, then you can perhaps give more hopeful news.'

Russell groaned. 'I can't even help in the theatre, I've had far too much to drink.'

'It wouldn't be a good idea and you know it, so don't waste time in regrets. Can you drive or shall I call a taxi?'

'No thanks, I didn't mean I was unfit to drive. Thank you, Sir John, you're most considerate. Will you explain to the Croftons for me, please, and give my excuses, they'll need a lift or a taxi as I brought them.'

'And Miss Tremaine? Can I get you a taxi?'

'Fleur will come with me, thank you. I won't be able to do anything useful at Chad's, so I can take her home as soon as I've made that phone call.'

Without another word he turned and, as if unaware that he still had his arm about Fleur's waist, led her out to the car. Lady Summers stood ready with Fleur's cloak, which she draped across her shoulders when they reached the front door.

'Look after him, my dear,' she whispered. 'He'll take it hard if she's badly hurt, or worse. He's very fond of her.'

ELEVEN

Fleur sat beside Russell on that nightmare drive back to Chad's, her feelings alternating wildly as if on some crazy, out of control merry-go-round. She was concerned for Rowena, as she would have been for anyone badly injured. She thought of her as a patient, not her rival for Russell's love. She glanced at him. It was clear from the grim set of his face, and the speed at which he drove, that he had thoughts only for the girl he was hurrying towards. He must love her very much.

As for Fleur's feelings towards Russell, she veered between anger that he should involve her, so cruelly insisting that she accompany him when he rushed to see his injured fiancée, and terror that he would crash his car or be stopped for speeding.

It was natural he should go to Chad's, but to force her along too was a kind of desertion, when he had been pretending he still loved her. This hurt more than if he had sent her home. To be compelled to see his concern, to watch him agonise over the injuries of the woman he really loved, would strain her endurance to the uttermost.

She had to fight down her uncharitable desire to tell him he was despicable, but she knew she would do as he wished. If he needed it, she would provide comfort. It was impossible to challenge him now, whatever cruelty he was subjecting her to.

Fleur took little notice of the other traffic, apart from vaguely thinking it was busy so near Christmas, and dreading to see the flashing blue lights of a police car behind them. She was surprised when they swept past the Houses of Parliament to see that it was still only eleven o'clock. It had seemed an endless time since Russell had appeared on her doorstep and, to avoid a quarrel in front of the Croftons, she had meekly gone with him to the party.

She flinched, but did not try to draw away when they reached Chad's and Russell, parking as near to the front entrance as he could, took her hand and drew her after him. He went straight to the lifts and up to the theatre suite at the top of the building.

'Please, will you wait there, darling?' he said, nodding towards a small room opposite the lifts.

She stared after him with a surge of fury. How dared he call her darling when it was perfectly obvious that all his love and concern were for the girl at present the centre of attention in the big operating theatre, where a subdued bustle indicated skilled, urgent, but quiet and controlled action.

He disappeared into the theatre sister's office, and with a shrug Fleur turned and went into the room he had pointed to. It was a small waiting room, with a few hard chairs and a pile of old magazines. A large man dressed in shabby old trousers and a dirty, oil-stained anorak, under which Fleur could see an even dirtier sweater, was slumped into one of the chairs, his eyes closed, but his hands gripped tightly together in front of him.

At the sound of Fleur's high heels he stood up quickly, then seeing how she was dressed subsided back onto the chair. But she could feel his eyes upon her when she sat down and listlessly picked up a copy of Vogue, and wondered dully why he was there.

Suddenly he spoke, with a broad Yorkshire accent, and she realised that he was very close to breaking down.

'I 'adn't a chance, true as I sit 'ere! The car slewed right round and straight into me, I swear it did!'

Fleur looked up at him slowly. 'Were you driving the lorry?' she asked. He nodded and bit his lip.

'I've never 'ad no accident, clean record for ten year,' he said. 'And now, she's—' He suddenly frowned, and looked closely at Fleur. 'Are you a friend, or a sister?' he asked fearfully, inclining his head towards the theatre.

Fleur shook her head quickly. 'No. I was with...a friend of hers when we got the news, and he's gone along to find out what's happening. He's a surgeon. She works here, as a secretary, did you know that?'

'Aye. Mayhap they'll pull 'er through, but that bloke, the tall thin 'un, didn't seem to 'old out much 'ope.'

'That's one of the senior surgeons,' Fleur said, recognising Mr Havelock from his description. 'He's very good, and if anyone

179

can help her he can, so don't worry, she's in good hands.'

'It weren't my fault, I knows that, but if—if the lass dies I'd not know 'ow to live wi' it,' he said slowly. 'I couldn't drive a lorry again, and it's th' only thing I can do.'

'We don't know yet how badly hurt she is, so don't imagine the worst. As for driving, it must be like riding a horse, or a bike. The sooner you get back on after a fall the better it is.'

He gave her the ghost of a smile, then fell silent again, but a nervous tic showed in his cheek, and after a few minutes Fleur said quietly that she was going to find some tea.

Her own ward was close so she went down to the kitchen. After a word to the staff nurse on duty she made two strong sweet mugs of tea. She wondered whether to make one for Russell, but she had no idea how long he would be, and in any case he could get some from the theatre kitchen if he wished.

It felt decidedly odd and uncomfortable to be in the familiar ward in party clothes, and she was glad to finish. The lorry driver accepted his mug with a blank stare, then looked up at her and nodded his thanks.

'Ta, lass. Just the ticket. 'Ow did you find this?'

'I'm a nurse here,' she said briefly.

'You'll look after 'er, won't you?' he asked with a childlike simplicity, and Fleur realised that Rowena would be in her ward, and no doubt she would have to watch Russell visiting her every day. Rubbing the salt in, she thought with numb resignation.

Then she heard footsteps coming briskly along the corridor, and voices. The door was pushed further open and one of the theatre nurses, carrying a tray of mugs, came into the room. She was followed by Russell. Fleur did not hear the nurse's exclamation that they had already got tea, both she and the lorry driver were on their feet, looking anxiously at Russell. He was tense, but not so bleak as before.

'She's come through,' he said quietly. 'It's too early yet to tell whether there'll be any permanent effect, but Mr Havelock is hopeful, there's just a hairline fracture and no other apparent damage to her head. And the abdominal injuries seem very minor, although she's got a slightly perforated gut. I'd better go and phone her mother. She'll be getting really distraught by now, it's hours after Rowena should have got home.'

He turned swiftly and left. Fleur sat down abruptly.

'I went and made tea,' she explained.

'Of course, you're on female surgical, aren't you?' the other nurse exclaimed. 'I was trying to think where I'd seen you before, people look so different out of uniform, don't they?' Then she turned to the lorry driver. 'Can you manage another? I expect you'll want to be getting on home now.'

He shuddered. 'I can't drive the lorry,' he said hastily.

'Why not, is it too badly damaged?' the nurse asked.

'No, 'ardly dented the front wing, just—I can't!'

'From what I heard the accident wasn't in any way your fault, and if the police don't want you to stay oughtn't you be getting home? Are you on the phone?'

He nodded, puzzled. 'The police as 'ow they'd be in touch, they 'ad my statement earlier. I just 'ad to stay till I knew...' he tailed off and gave a sudden gasp of relief. 'Thank God she's not dead!'

'Of course,' the nurse said soothingly. 'Now when you get home, telephone and ask how she is. If you leave your number I'll see to it someone rings you in the morning too. Look, come down with me now and I'll arrange it all.'

She shepherded him out of the room and Fleur was left alone, wondering whether she ought to call for a taxi. Russell would certainly prefer to stay at Chad's, and now Rowena was, for the moment at any rate, out of danger, he no longer needed Fleur for the very odd kind of support he seemed to demand of her.

She gave a deep, shuddering sigh, then rose and left the room. There was nothing to tell her where Russell was, but she thought he was most likely in the theatre nurse's office using her phone. She went down in the lift and the porter, eyeing her curiously, telephoned for a taxi. He found her a pencil and a sheet of paper and she wrote a hurried note to Russell, which the porter promised to give him.

'Don't worry now, I'm here all night, and won't miss him. I'll see he gets it straight away.'

To Fleur's relief the taxi came almost immediately and by now the traffic had thinned so that she was home and in bed in a very short time. Exhausted, she slept, and woke only to the sound of her alarm a few hours later.

Hastening to Chad's she had little time to think about the previous night, but there was a deep shadow over everything, and she thought she could never be happy again.

Rowena was in the ward, in the bed nearest the office, where a close watch could be kept on her.

'She's still drowsy, but her pulse and temperature are stable, and she seems to be holding her own,' Sister Reynolds told Fleur. 'Mr Delaney asked me to tell you that he was enormously grateful for your support last night, and he'll be round some time this morning. I believe he went to fetch Mrs Kingsley, for she doesn't drive and Mr Kingsley's not due back until late this evening. What a shock for the poor man, at Christmas too, but the chances are she'll recover completely.'

By the afternoon Rowena was fully awake, and although very dazed and weak, seemed to understand where she was, and why. Mr Havelock came to see her, but no other visitors were allowed until Fleur was about to go off duty. She was leaving the ward when Russell came in, accompanied by a woman so like Rowena, despite her age, that she could only be her mother, and a tall young man with the same fair colouring, who must be her brother.

Fleur stepped back hurriedly, but Russell had seen her and while the other two went softly across the ward to where Rowena lay, he paused.

'I'll run you home as soon as I can get away,' he said quietly. 'I'm so sorry yesterday evening was ruined, but I understood you preferred to get home after the operation.'

Fleur looked after him in amazement as he crossed to where the curtains were now drawn about Rowena's bed. What on earth could they have to say to one another? Then she reflected that if she wanted to avoid him she had better move quickly. She changed rapidly into a thick warm skirt, and a soft angora wool sweater of a delicate rose shade. She was about to leave when it occurred to her that even if she evaded Russell at the hospital, he was quite capable of following her home.

She could not face the thought of a showdown with him. Not tonight, when she was so tired and still distraught, and had not had time to think about his odd actions. She could not go home yet, and she sighed wearily. Where could she be safe from Russell's inexplicable behaviour for a few hours?

Suddenly she remembered Jenny's request. Of course, she would go across to the nurses' hostel and stay in Jenny's room. Anxiously she searched her bag and sighed in relief. She had the key. She could wait there until it was safe to go home. She could even sleep there, she thought, for there was no knowing when Russell might appear or telephone and to be constantly on the alert would be almost as bad as facing him.

She went swiftly to the hostel, casting anxious glances about her. There was no sign of Russell, however, and she ran up the stairs to the third floor where Jenny had a room, number 326.

The hostel was an old building, originally several large terraced houses which had been converted, with newer wings sticking out at the back. It was a maze of corridors, and Fleur had to pause several times to read the room numbers. She was standing near one sign which had partly torn, trying to make out whether the last number was a five or a six when she heard a familiar voice in the corridor round the corner.

For a few seconds she thought it must be a nurse she knew, then her eyes snapped wide open in astonishment, and she turned to face the girl approaching along the other corridor.

'Hello, Liza,' she said quietly, and Liza Price almost dropped her bag in surprise. 'How is St John's these days?' Fleur went on, looking at the girl with Liza. For a moment she could not place her, then the embarrassed hostility in her eyes made Fleur recall the time when she had taken the girl, Gilly Massingham, to task for carelessness.

Liza recovered rapidly. 'Why, Nurse Flirt,' she exclaimed, a gleeful expression in her voice. 'Fancy seeing you. I thought you might be out with the fantastic concussion case. Or has he tired of you and gone back to the Monarch's daughter?'

Fleur pressed her lips tightly together. She would not allow Liza to provoke her into any unwise comments. Instead she smiled slightly, and merely stared enquiringly at Gilly.

'Someone has soon been busy with the

gossip. Have you come to visit London, Liza? And how do you two know each other?'

'Liza's my cousin,' Gilly explained, and Fleur saw a look of slight annoyance on Liza's face.

Suddenly she understood how the rumours had come to Chad's, and been exaggerated into much nastier stories. Liza's old jealousy, plus Gilly's resentment at being reprimanded by someone she regarded as a newcomer to Chad's, and the unfortunate coincidence that the two were cousins, explained it all.

'Lucky you,' she said lightly. 'Have a good time in London, Liza. I must go now, and decide which of the ten invitations I've received I shall accept tonight.'

'Well!' she heard Liza exclaim in astonished fury, but she had turned and walked away down the corridor.

Fleur let herself into Jenny's room quickly. She slowly took off her coat and sank down in the chair. So Russell wasn't the author of the rumours after all. In that she'd maligned him. But it didn't mean she had been wrong about his other behaviour, she told herself fiercely. He was deceitful, hurtful and totally unscrupulous.

She hoped that he sat outside her flat all night if he had the nerve to want to go on pretending that everything was well between them, while all the time he had been using her to make Rowena jealous.

She would find it very difficult to nurse Rowena properly, she thought, whatever professionalism she called to her aid. But she must, as she must steel herself to see Russell, not only in the ward as a surgeon, but also as Rowena's fiancé. And she must endure knowing looks, or sympathetic glances, both equally difficult to bear, when the Chad's grapevine had been at work and her colleagues learned of the new twists of the affair.

She spent the night tossing and turning, wondering what Russell had done. It was almost worse not to know, she told herself crossly, than it would have been facing him. But today she must, and she still had to finish the painting and wallpapering in the flat.

Rowena was awake, but rather drowsy, and Fleur found it possible to conceal her feelings as she worked. Russell visited while she was at lunch, and the couple who had been before, Rowena's mother and brother, came in the afternoon when

Fleur was busy with another patient who had just come down from the theatre after having a broken ankle dealt with.

She was walking down the ward a couple of hours later, about to go off duty when there was a slight scream from the first year student. Fleur was nearest her, and she grabbed the girl as she ran distractedly towards sister's office.

'What is it?' she demanded. 'Control yourself, nurse!'

'Miss Kingsley,' the student babbled. 'Quick, do something, she's bleeding, the wound in her stomach's bleeding awfully fast! She'll bleed to death!'

TWELVE

Fleur flew across to Rowena's bed, flinging instructions over her shoulder as she went. She was standing beside Rowena, the blankets tossed aside, applying pressure to the newly gaping wound when Sister wheeled a trolley across to the bed.

'Something warm, a hot towel,' Fleur ordered, and the student, who had recovered a measure of calm, ran to find one.

Fleur had probed the wound gently and discovered a ruptured artery, and was pinching the ends together to stop the flow of blood. She pressed the towel over the wound and her hand, while Sister rearranged the blanket across Rowena's legs. Both knew that direct warmth would help the coagulation, and Sister sent the student nurse to fetch more towels.

When the emergency doctor appeared, Fleur was concentrating so hard on what she was doing that she barely noticed it was Russell who had appeared at her side.

He swiftly applied clamps while Sister reported what had happened, then spoke quietly to Fleur.

'Keep those in place while we transfer her to theatre.'

Fleur nodded, he and Sister carefully transferred Rowena to a trolley, and she walked beside it as they went to the lift.

'Scrub up and help me, please, Fleur, we're short staffed,' Russell ordered as the anaesthetist began to work on Rowena, and Fleur nodded wordlessly, then rapidly prepared for theatre.

She worked with him in utter absorption, swabbing, handing him instruments, then threading needles for him first to sew up the artery, then once more to close the operation wound.

When Rowena had been taken back to the ward Fleur felt free to go home. She was drained, both from the nervous energy always expended when there was such a crisis, and her emotions as she had watched Russell straining to save the life of the girl he loved. Some aloof part of her admired his skill, and worked with dedication to provide all the assistance he needed, while a different part of her mind was numb with despair, knowing all was over between them. Whatever little there had ever been, she reminded herself wearily as she waited for the bus, peering to see its light through a thick fog which had developed during the day.

Russell, to her relief, had merely spoken quickly to her as she had left the theatre.

'Rowena's father is due here in an hour or so. I must stay to put him in the picture, so forgive me if I can't see you again tonight. If it's not too late after he gets here I may be able to phone you, but I'll see you tomorrow.'

Late as it was when she got home, Fleur spent an hour painting, longing for his call, yet dreading it. What could they say? If Russell had been intending to amuse himself with her while they were both on duty over the Christmas holiday, and Rowena was safely at home, this was now completely changed. He would certainly wish to spend all his spare time with Rowena, and be in no mood for cynical, casual love-making with another woman.

Christmas Eve was especially busy for Fleur. They were working with the minimum of staff over the holiday. The ward was half empty, which helped reduce the regular workload, but the need for frequent observations on Rowena's condition, the transfusion and monitoring of fluid balance, and then the care of another emergency patient who was brought in with jaundice, stretched them to the uttermost.

Mr Kingsley's plane had been delayed by the fog, Fleur heard, and was expected later that day. But Rowena was making rapid progress, and would be out of danger within days. She was very weak, but taking notice of what went on. She smiled wanly when Russell came in to see her, and clung to his hand to retain him when he moved to leave.

Fleur had avoided him, dodging into the sluice when she saw him enter the ward, and then making an excuse to go on an errand to the pharmacy before he was able to detach himself from Rowena's possessive clasp. On returning she remained out of sight until he had seen his other patients and left the ward.

As she was about to go for lunch an hour later Sister Reynolds came up to her with a worried frown on her face.

'My dear, night sister is off sick, gastric flu, and I need to rearrange the rota, but we're desperately short staffed. Would it be possible for you to go off now and report back for night duty this evening? I need someone reliable in charge, and you're the most senior staff nurse I've got during Christmas.'

'Of course,' Fleur said at once. She knew how difficult it would be to make satisfactory arrangements at the present time.

'I've already tried the agencies but all their staff are covering for holidays,' Sister said apologetically. 'I hope it doesn't spoil your plans. Can you sleep this afternoon? I'll stay and cover till then, so you'll have time for eight hours.'

'I can sleep in Jenny's room,' Fleur said quickly. 'I've got her key, as I'm looking after her plants, so there's no need for me to go home. I'll be quite relieved not to,' she added, glancing out of the windows where the fog had become even more dense. And Russell could not contact her, she thought.

The ward was exceptionally quiet when Sister Reynolds handed over to her. All the patients were asleep, and the noise of the traffic was muted by the fog. When several church bells rang out at midnight Fleur jumped slightly, it was so unexpected.

An hour later she was helping the junior nurse to turn one of the elderly patients when a slight noise by the doorway caused her to glance over her shoulder, then with a quiet word to the other girl she went swiftly along the ward.

Mr Kingsley, looking indescribably weary, stood there with the tall blond man Fleur had seen before. He nodded slightly to Fleur and looked round anxiously for his daughter.

'She's much better,' Fleur said softly. 'Over here.'

She led them to Rowena's bed, and as they looked down at the sleeping girl, Fleur touched him lightly on the arm.

'I'll make you coffee, and you can read her notes in my office,' she suggested, and he threw her a brief, grateful smile.

A few minutes later she was pouring three cups of coffee from a large jug, and handing the two men a plate of biscuits. Mr Kingsley sipped his coffee, and visibly relaxed.

'Thank you Staff Nurse Tremaine. I needed that. My plane was diverted to Elmdon because of the fog and I've had a horrendous journey by coach down the M1. There were no trains being Christmas Eve, and no cars for hire. Thank goodness Peter was able to meet me at Victoria. Do you know Peter Burroughs?'

The tall young man smiled at her and held out his hand.

'We haven't met formally,' he said in a deep, attractive voice, 'but Russell told me how much I owe you, he said Rowena might not have pulled through if you hadn't taken such prompt action yesterday. We both owe you a great deal.'

Fleur was confused. So he was not Rowena's brother, she was thinking. Who was he? Could he be a friend of the family? And who did he mean by that 'both'? Had he referred to himself and Mr Kingsley, and if so why, or had he been including Russell, and if so again why? In what way were they associated?

Her reflections were interrupted as Mr Kingsley, intently reading his daughter's notes, asked a few questions and then, draining his cup of coffee, shook his head when she offered more.

'Thank you, but no. I can see Rowena is in good hands, and I must get some sleep. Peter will drive me home and we'll come in later this afternoon. Goodnight, my dear. Tell Russell I've been, when I phoned him he told me he was on call and said he'd pop in during the night. Are you ready, Peter?'

'Yes, indeed. Thank you, Staff Nurse Tremaine. I can quite see why Russell is so taken with you.'

By now thoroughly bewildered, Fleur watched them leave, then turned her attentions to writing up some notes. It was difficult to concentrate, and after a fruitless half hour she went round the ward, checking everything, then handed over to the floating auxiliary nurse while she went for a meal. When she returned she was unsure whether to be sorry or relieved to find that Russell had paid his promised visit during her absence.

'Mr Delaney seemed pleased with Miss Kingsley's progress,' the nurse reported. 'I told him her father had been in to see her, and he said to call him if there was any change.'

The rest of the night was peaceful, but Fleur was exhausted when she handed over. Sister Reynolds eyed her with concern.

'I do wish I hadn't had to ask you to do the night duty,' she said apologetically, 'but night sister is better and insists she'll be OK tonight, so go and sleep now, have a good Christmas dinner, and I'll see you back here tomorrow morning as usual. Two more days and you can forget it all while you celebrate New Year. I'll be thankful for a break myself.'

The fog was still thick, and Fleur was sleepily emerging from the main doors before she realised that there would be very few buses on Christmas morning. She sighed wearily. If it had been a bright frosty morning she would have enjoyed a brisk walk home, but it would be damp and depressing in this weather.

She took a few steps foward, then jumped nervously as a hand grasped her arm.

'The car's over here,' Russell said, and she permitted him to help her in, too weary to protest.

He drove slowly, for the fog drifted in confusing eddies and it was sometimes difficult to tell where they were going. Russell spoke no more, and Fleur could think of nothing to say until he swung into a driveway and stopped outside a tall, brick building she did not recognise.

'Where's this?' she asked, rousing herself from the lassitude that had possessed her. 'It's not the flat.'

'I live here. You're going to sleep in my spare room, I can't trust you not to wear yourself out painting all day and all night, if I let you go,' was the astonishing reply.

'I can't!' Fleur protested, but he ignored her, came to open her door, and she knew that she would be unable to resist him. Part of her mind clung to every last second in his company, despite the knowledge that she would only be hurt more by it.

He led her into an expensively carpeted foyer, greeted a uniformed porter, and guided Fleur into a lift. It shot rapidly to the top floor. Inside the flat was a large hallway, and through wide double doors she could see a bright, high ceilinged living room with deep leather chairs at one end, and on a raised dais at the other a dining table and chairs.

The room had a spacious but lived in air. There was a thick white carpet and brightly patterned rugs. Books lined one wall, an elaborate stereo system another, and at both ends long green velvet curtains concealed what must be huge windows. Russell opened another door on the opposite side of the hall.

'The kitchen's through there,' he said briefly, indicating another door. 'Help yourself if you need anything. That's my room, and as much as I'd appreciate your company, my sweet, I'm prescribing eight hours sleep,' he went on, drawing her into a large twin bedded room decorated in a delicate shade of blue. 'Then breakfast in bed and a long soak in the tub. Your bathroom's through there and you'll find a robe and some new toothbrushes, though no nightdresses, I'm afraid,' he added with a grin. 'Later we'll have a quiet dinner. I've arranged for one to be sent up from the restaurant here. Sleep well, my darling.'

He was gone, the door closing gently behind him, and Fleur pinched herself.

She was not dreaming, unless one could feel pain in a dream, she decided, and then, too weary to try and sort it out, she hastened to make ready and fall into one of the inviting looking beds.

She awoke hours later as the door clicked to. There was a delicious fragrance of coffee, and as she tried to think how she came to be in this strange bed she turned her head to see a tray, with orange juice, coffee and toast, on the bedside table.

She sat up, discovered her nakedness, and as recollection flooded back thought gratefully of Russell's tact in not waiting in the room until she awoke. Revitalised by the deep sleep, she was soon relaxing in the bath, enjoying the unashamed luxury of the thickly carpeted, fully tiled bathroom, which she had barely noticed the night before, and the circular bath.

Regretting that she had no clean clothes, only the old blue woollen skirt with matching sweater that she had worn the previous two days, she dressed. Then, with some trepidation, for she was so confused by Russell's actions that she had no idea what she was going to say to him, she went into the living room.

He was sitting in one of the armchairs,

glancing at a copy of the Lancet, but he sprang up and came forward to pull her into his arms and kiss her lingeringly.

'You looked like a child, snuggled up in bed,' he said with a rather uneven laugh as he finally released her. 'It took all my resolution to leave the room. Happy Christmas, my darling. Come and sit beside me.'

How could he behave as though he loved her, as if Rowena did not exist, she thought with a sudden spurt of annoyance. Then the memory of her night duty returned, with its further puzzles.

'Who is Peter Burroughs?' Fleur asked as he pulled her down onto a settee, his arm around her shoulders.

'Peter? We were at a school together. Why do you want to know about him?'

'He came last night, with Mr Kingsley, and I had assumed when I saw him with Rowena's mother earlier that he was her brother.'

Russell laughed. 'Oh, no. He and Rowena are engaged.'

Fleur sat abruptly upright. She must be dreaming!

'He's engaged to Rowena?' she almost squeaked.

'That's what I said. Why are you so surprised? Why shouldn't he be?'

'But—but you are!' she said faintly.

He stared at her in astonishment.

'Why on earth should you think that? Did you believe that silly rumour? There was nothing in that. I've never been engaged to Rowena, and would never wish to be. Is that why you've been so cold these last few days,' he went on slowly, 'why you've seemed so bewildered? Did you really think that I would be taking you out, and making it so plain that I loved you, if I were engaged to someone else?'

A warm glow was spreading through Fleur's limbs. There were still some things she did not understand, though.

'I couldn't entirely believe that you were pretending,' she said slowly. 'Yet from all I'd heard it seemed—well, as though you were either heartless, or very skilled at pretending, so that you had deceived me!'

'My reputation!' he groaned. 'And those wretched rumours! But I'd have thought you knew better than to believe all the rumours you hear at Chad's after what they said about you.'

Fleur smiled up at him. 'Your fault,'

she accused fondly. 'At the time I could cheerfully have forgotten all about trying to save life, and murdered you! I'm still wondering why Sister Beasley never reported me.'

'Oh, didn't I tell you?'

She looked puzzled.

'What could you have had to do with it?' she asked.

He grinned, and took both her hands in his.

'Just a precaution,' he murmured, holding her tightly. 'I had an inexplicable recurrence of my concussion,' he said reminiscently, his eyes gleaming with laughter. 'Much against my normal inclinations, I assure you, unless I was delirious and thought she was you, I somehow found myself kissing Sister. Thank heavens Chad's grapevine never got hold of that, or the rumour would have had me so desperate that I needed to restore my ego by taking out every nurse that enters the place!'

After an astonished gasp, Fleur suddenly giggled.

'No wonder she went off duty, and didn't report me,' she giggled. 'You devil! But thank you, rather belatedly.'

'You owe me a few kisses in compensation,' he warned, and proceeded to collect a few of them.

Much later, he spoke. 'What else, apart from rumour, gave you the idea that I was engaged to Rowena?'

'It was something else,' Fleur said slowly, her mind in a whirl, 'something which I didn't think could be explained away. I came into her office a few days ago, when she was in Mr Havelock's room. I overheard her saying she was sorry, asking for another chance. Then you came out of the room, but you didn't see me, and when Rowena came out she looked so happy. She'd been in a dreadful temper before that, everyone assumed it was because her engagement to you had been broken off.'

'Her engagement, but not to me, had been broken. She was telephoning Peter. I was there because I had bullied her into making the first move. They're both stubborn as mules, and someone had to to something.'

Fleur took a deep breath. 'I see, but why should it matter to you? And you were so concerned, when you heard she'd been injured, and you came to see her so often, and when she had that relapse, I—I was sure you loved her! Why were you so involved? Just because Peter is a friend of yours?'

'A little more. I'm very fond of her and was concerned on my own account. Rowena's my cousin, you see. Her mother and mine are sisters.'

'No-one at Chad's knows that,' she said slowly.

'We didn't advertise that fact when I came to Chad's, because I couldn't endure it to be thought that any promotions I received might be due to my relationship with Mr Kingsley. Now are you willing to believe that I love you, my darling, and only you? And I don't wish to be engaged to anyone but you? In fact, I'm not too sure I want to be engaged at all, I'd far sooner be married!'

Fleur, for a very satisfactory reason, was unable to reply to this. His kisses had never been so sweet, and at last she could abandon herself to the joy of responding fervently to his lips as they explored hers. She could forget all her doubts, and accept the incredible fact that he loved her.

It was some considerable time later, while Fleur was laughingly and somewhat breathlessly trying to persuade Russell that much as she wanted to marry him that very day as he wished, it was impracticable, that a ring on the doorbell announced the arrival of the Christmas dinner Russell had ordered.

Fleur tried desperately to smooth her ruffled hair as the trolley was wheeled in, then Russell produced a bottle of champagne and poured two glasses.

'Happy Christmas,' he said softly.

'Oh, my present is at the flat,' Fleur remembered, dismayed.

'It can wait, you're my best ever Christmas gift. And I have to confess that I've no Christmas present for you yet, my sweet, but I want to buy you a pendant to match your engagement ring, as soon as the shops open. Then I'm driving you home to make wedding plans with your parents. To us, my darling. May we have many more Christmasses together.'

This Large Print Book for the Partially sighted, who cannot read normal print, is published under the auspices of

THE ULVERSCROFT FOUNDATION

THE ULVERSCROFT FOUNDATION

. . . we hope that you have enjoyed this Large Print Book. Please think for a moment about those people who have worse eyesight problems than you . . . and are unable to even read or enjoy Large Print, without great difficulty.

You can help them by sending a donation, large or small to:

**The Ulverscroft Foundation,
1, The Green, Bradgate Road,
Anstey, Leicestershire, LE7 7FU,
England.**
or request a copy of our brochure for more details.

The Foundation will use all your help to assist those people who are handicapped by various sight problems and need special attention.

Thank you very much for your help.